The Martian Wave
March 2024

Features

Short Stories

Flash Fiction

Poems

Illustrations

THE STAFF OF THE MARTIAN WAVE

EDITOR: Tyree Campbell
WEBMASTER: H David Blalock
COVER DESIGN: Marcia A. Borell, Laura Givens

First Printing September 2023
Hiraeth Publishing
http://hiraethsffh.com/
@HiraethPublish1

Cover art and design by Marcia A. Borell

Vol. V, No. 1   March 2024
The Martian Wave is published two times a year on the 1st days of March and September in the United States of America by Hiraeth Publishing, P.O. Box 1248, Tularosa, NM, 88352. Copyright 2024 by Hiraeth Publishing. All rights revert to authors and artists upon publication except as noted in selected individual contracts. Writers and artists guidelines are available online at www.hiraethsffh.com. Guidelines are also available upon request from Hiraeth Publishing, P.O. Box 1248, Tularosa, NM, 88352, if request is accompanied by a self-addressed #10 envelope with a first-class US stamp. Editor: Tyree Campbell.

A Little Help, Please

In the world of the small indie press we fight a never-ending battle for attention to our work, as writers and in publishing. Here's an example: big publishers [you know who they are] have gobs of $$$ that they can devote to advertising and marketing. Here at Hiraeth Publishing, our advertising budget consists of the deposits for whatever soda bottles and aluminum cans we can find alongside the highways. Anti-littering laws make our task even more difficult . . . ☺

That's where YOU come in. YOU are our best promoter. YOU are the one who can tell others about us. Just send 'em to our website, tell them about our store. That's all. Just that.

Of course, we don't mind if you talk us up. We're pretty good, you know. We have some award-winning and award-nominated writers and artists, plus other voices well-deserving to be heard [not everyone wins awards, right?] but our publications are read-worthy nevertheless.

That number once again is:

www.hiraethsffh.com

Friend us on Facebook at Hiraeth Publishing
Follow us on Twitter at @HiraethPublish1

TYREE CAMPBELL
BECOMING JADE

Annae (real name Maryjade) is an assassin sent to Deege, a forested world, to kill a plant and bring back the druzy who carries it. Druzies resemble young girls, but seem to have no life and no purpose but to act as transportation to the plants. In the process, Annae loses contact with her own spacecraft and is marooned on the world.

The man who hired Annae for this task is also responsible for the death of Annae's twin sister. Annae has accepted this contract because it presents an opportunity to kill the killer. However, the loss of the twin has crippled Annae. She is virtually unable to communicate with anyone, except in the course of negotiating her contracts. She has taken to talking with the memory of her dead sister, and with no one else.

Now, marooned on Deege, she must find a way to break out of her isolation and communicate with the druzies, and with a strange young woman who cannot speak, or she will be compelled to remain on this world forever.

https://www.hiraethsffh.com/product-page/becoming-jade-by-tyree-campbell

What???
No subscription to
The Martian Wave??

We can fix that . . .

The Martian Wave is published three times a year, in March, July, and November. It contains science fiction, fantasy, and some dark fiction short stories, poems, articles, reviews, and art, mostly centered on the exploration and settlement of other worlds. We offer one- and two-year subscriptions. Go to the link below and order. Simple.

https://www.hiraethsffh.com/product-page/martian-wave

And remember: a subscription makes a great gift, for a holiday or birthday or any time of the year!

Pyra and the Tektites

Pyra, age thirteen, is running away from home in the Asteroid Belt because she's not doing well in school. Her parents want to send her to Mars for school, and she doesn't want to go. She sneaks aboard a cargo shuttle, and falls asleep in the hold. When she awakens, she finds herself in free-fall; the shuttle has been seized by the Tektites, a group of rebel pirates—

. . . and the adventures begin!

https://www.hiraethsffh.com/product-page/pyra-and-the-tektites-by-tyree-campbell

The Sisterhood of the Blood Moon
By Terrie Leigh Relf

For thousands of Earth years, the Transgalactic Consortium has had an invested interest in this planet and its inhabitants, the Haurans. While the Sisterhood of the Blood Moon and the Guardians work together with the Consortium and Haurans to restore balance to the universe, the Blood Moon is fast approaching. The power of this moon reveals untold secrets . . . including the sacred covenant with the Mora Spiders. There is an ancient pact that continues to be honored – but at what cost and for whose purpose?

The world may come to an end. But will there be a chance for a new beginning? And if so, where?

https://www.hiraethsffh.com/product-page/sisterhood-of-the-blood-moon-by-terrie-leigh-relf

INDIGO
By Tyree Campbell

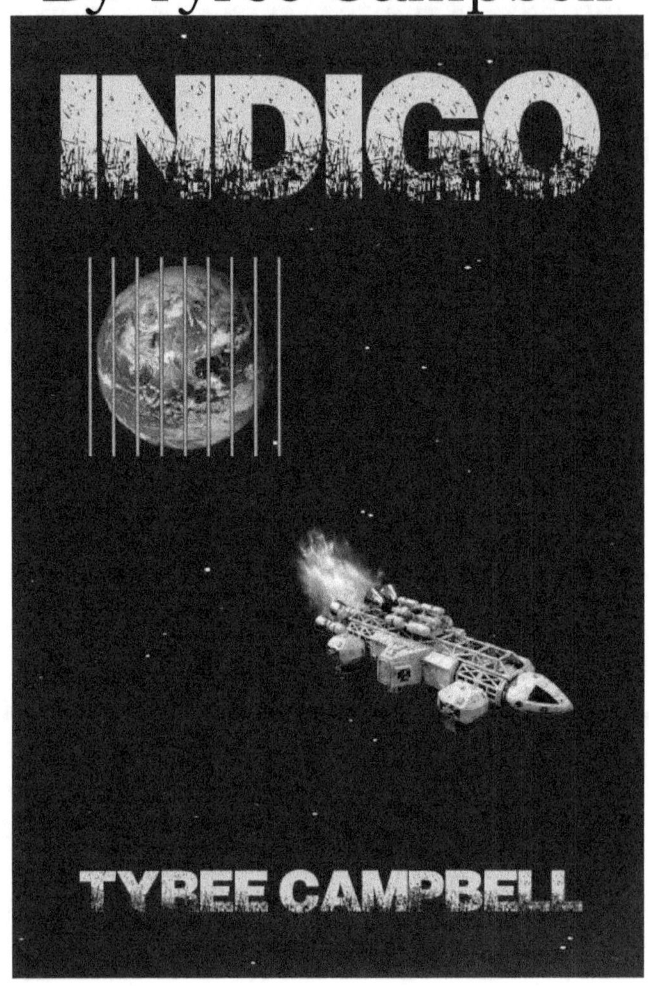

Matt has a special gift that will enable him to avenge his brother's death. Kerise has another use for that talent, if only she can persuade him to abandon his personal quest and help her with a project called Indigo.

Echelon, a secret government project, also wants Matt because of his gift. But as he and other like him cannot be controlled, they pose a threat to national security. Orders go out to have them eliminated.

Interpol is on the lookout for Kerise and for the Indigo project. There is no place on Earth where Matt and Kerise and her associates will be safe. Nowhere on Earth...but they cannot be safe unless Matt commits himself to Indigo. And he's not about to do that...

https://www.hiraethsffh.com/product-page/indigo-by-tyree-campbell

The Spark
By Stephen C. Curro

Katrina grew up in a frigid world ruled by a tyrant. By day, she works as a mechanic. At night, she becomes the Ace, the King's personal assassin. She's not proud of her job, but she's accepted that it's the way things are. At least she has her boyfriend Dez and his little brother Uriah to light her life.

When Katrina is ordered to quash a rebel attack on the King's Command Center, she thinks it's just another job. But as she uncovers the plot, she is shocked to learn that Dez may be involved with the dissidents. Now Katrina must make an impossible choose—eliminate the one she loves, or defy the King she swore to serve.

The Spark is a sci-fi thriller about love, betrayal, and how the futures of others, even a whole civilization, can be determined through a single choice.

https://www.hiraethsffh.com/product-page/the-spark-by-stephen-c-curro

The Empty Planet
Elana Gomel

The first child disappeared on the night of the Small Moon. The parents were instantly arrested. They were Settlers, part of the group of the cryogenically frozen free riders who had been pulled out of storage when the aging *Hope* limped to its final destination after the grueling journey of 300 years. Only twenty-three people out of the original hundred were successfully revived; the rest had shrunk into ice mummies.

The ten thousand Colonists, descendants of the ten generations of ship-born and bred, regarded the Settlers with fear and disgust Everything their ancestors had fled from had been thawed out with the Settlers: languages no one understood; gods no one worshipped; and science no one had any interest in. And with the disappearance of little Andrew, the ancient history of infanticide on the dying Earth had become hot news, the crime for Sheriff Song Chantea to solve and for the Captain and Council to punish. So, Chantea quickly locked up the missing baby's parents David and Maria Hughes in the town's new prefab jail and declared the case closed.

However, when the second child was gone during the next Small Moon, blaming the parents was no longer an option. They were Colonists, trustworthy and reliable, members of the Council. And their story of what had happened was almost identical to the Hughes': the baby left sleeping in the cot, the parents stepping out for fresh air for a couple of minutes and coming back to find the cot empty. Sheriff Song offered carefully worded reassurances but decided to keep the Settler parents in jail a while longer.

Captain Nassrin Elabouni listened in silence until Song finished her report. Then both women looked simultaneously out the window, as if daring their new home to solve the riddle for them.

The view was, frankly, boring: a flat yellowish-tan plain, crisscrossed with meandering streams. The dull light of Gliese 18 made the water gleam like black metal. The star was dimmer than the Sol. The Settlers often complained that its light felt inadequate, as if filtered through an old dusty lampshade, but the Colonists, tired of the artificial brightness of the *Hope*'s AI-controlled diurnal cycle, embraced it wholeheartedly. The monotony of the bare earth was broken only by an occasional rocky outcrop and patches of velvety black and purple along the watercourses. These were Omnia's equivalent of lichens and algae, taking the first hesitant steps onto the land. There were no other land plants and no animals, though Omnia's shallow landlocked seas had photosynthesizing organisms aplenty. They were squiggly plankton-like creatures, ranging in size from microscopic to visibly puny. They converted solar energy into chemical compounds but could also feed on each other. They were the15ecrean Omnia had enough oxygen for human beings to survive on its uninspiring surface of barren plains and low mountains. In fact, this very paucity of life was the reason the planet, originally nameless, had been chosen for the last-ditch desperate attempt at colonization.

Earth had been dying for a long time, ravaged by climate change and endless low-key military clashes like a chronically ill patient barely clinging to life but unwilling to let go. The Hope movement, arising out of the ashes of the Green parties, wanted to start anew. But FTL probes sent to nearby stars brought back pictures so bizarre that nobody could figure out what they showed. Were the forests of gleaming fluorescent spikes life-forms, artificial structures, or something else completely unimaginable? What about self-weaving nets that covered thousands of square miles with their slithery strands? The Universe was far stranger than humans could comprehend, and aliens were...well, alien. That was why the sheer boredom of Gliese 18-B, later named Omnia, meaning "plenty", was such a lure to the handful of people tired of the unpredictability and randomness of life on Earth. The original Colonists did not want to wait until the FTL drive, successfully used on small probes, could be developed to power large spaceships – if it ever could. They saw Earth turning into an alien planet, and they wanted an alien planet which they could mold into their image of the Earth of the past. Omnia, plain, empty, and safe, was a perfect canvass to paint their green dream on.

And now there seemed to be a menacing, if indecipherable, message scribbled on this canvass.

Nassrin tapped her fingers on the desk. She had been elected Captain after the Blackout, a catastrophic engine failure that happened during the approach to the system. Two hundred people died including the former Captain. Song Chantea had also run for captainship and lost. The role of Sheriff was a consolation prize.

Nassrin had been an unexpected choice, and in Chantea's private opinion, a wrong one. The ship's former Chaplain, she was widely respected for her calmness and deep knowledge of history. But, Chantea thought, she was not decisive enough to cope with new challenges. Fortunately, after the Blackout, everything had gone smoothly for the new colony. Both the planetfall and the building of the town went without a glitch, and Nassrin's peaceful demeanor seemed to be exactly what the people craved.

"So," Nassrin said, "why didn't you release the Settler couple? They could not have abducted the second baby."

The Hughes had been under lock and key when the Colonists Rhea and Dimitris Kolonaki found their baby daughter gone.

"What about the other Settlers?" Chantea countered.

"Why would they do such a thing?"

In the town of ten thousand people, laid out in a grid of small prefab houses and surrounded by green fields and solar plantations, everybody knew everybody's business. Babies, the colony's most precious possession, were registered, counted, medically supervised, and doted upon by every adult. It would be impossible for a nonpregnant couple to acquire a new baby without it becoming common knowledge within an hour.

"You know what they say," Chantea muttered.

Famines had been savage and unrelenting in the years before the *Hope*'s departure, and cannibalism had been widespread. Infanticide became a ritual for the "technos" who, having killed their planet, turned to their own children to satisfy their greed and lust for destruction. So the books and vids in the *Hope*'s archives claimed, and Chantea never doubted their veracity. Had it been up to her, the Settlers would have never been revived at all.

"Nobody needs to resort to cannibalism to eat," Nassrin retorted.

The Colonists had more food than they could use. Terrestrial crops thrived in the mineral-rich soil of Omnia; frozen embryos of rabbits and chickens had been successfully revived; and the agricultural district was a bright and growing splash of green in the middle of the desert. Their doctor Aker Jonasson reported that some Colonists needed to shed a couple of pounds – a condition unheard-of in generations.

"But some people are just evil," Chantea responded.

Nassrin shook her head.

"Talk to the Settler parents again," she said. "If they don't confess, let them go."

*   *   *

"Go fuck yourself," Dave Hughes said. His wife Maria stared into the distance; her face collapsed in upon itself as if she were eighty instead of thirty. Chantea observed them carefully, feeling goosebumps rise upon her wiry arms. She had never realized before how different the Settlers were, not just psychologically – she had never doubted this – but physically. It was not just their speech, with strange inflections and obscure words; not just their size – Dave towered over most Colonists whose frames had shrunk after generations in the artificial gravity and cramped quarters on the *Hope*. It was something wild and untamed in his rugged face; and something cold and sly in his wife's sullen grief.

17

"If you once again imply that we killed and ate our son," Dave continued in his booming voice, "I will make sure that you don't live long enough to see the real killer when we bring him in."

Chantea's fingers caressed the ribbed handle of her gun. Only eight had been printed and distributed to the colony's tiny police force of herself and her six deputies. One was given to Captain as the symbol of her authority, even though Nassrin seldom wore it. There was no need for firearms on Omnia, as there were no lifeforms except bacteria, lichens, and plankton-like squigglies, while the worst crime committed in the settlement until the abductions had been a drunken brawl.

"Threatening violence to prove you are not violent people?"

Maria stirred and looked Chantea in the face. She was taller and sturdier than the diminutive Sheriff. Maria's curly red hair, falling down in wild locks, reminded Chantea of the stories of *Ahps*, baby-snatching demons from Cambodian folklore, her father had told her when she was little. Now her father was dead, killed in the Blackout. Where was the justice in him dying, and these two living? They had been slumbering in their cryogenic cradles through the engine failure, while the Colonists struggled to save the *Hope*.

"Did you search our neighbors' house?" she asked. "They hate us. They could have taken Andrew out of spite."

When the prefabs had been distributed, Captain squashed the idea of having a separate precinct for the Settlers, insisting that they should live among Colonists. Chantea had objected then and felt some satisfaction in knowing she had been right.

"Hate you, really? Maybe you gave them a cause."

"It's useless," Dave muttered, turning to his wife. "They will never listen to us."

"I am not prejudiced. I investigate with open mind," Chantea responded. She had searched the Hughes' house but found nothing suspicious. The couple's story never varied. They had fed Andrew, put him in his cot where he fell asleep, and stepped outside into the yard to get a breath of fresh air and watch the brief transit of Omnia's tiny satellite. The satellite had a wildly elliptical orbit, and nights of the Small Moon were a flash of silver superseded by the velvety star-studded dark, which many Settlers found soothing.

When they went back in, the cot was empty.

"And you did not hear anything?"

Dave shook his head, but Maria hesitated.

"A whisper," she finally said. "Like...a ghost speaking, very faint."

"Why didn't you tell me this before?"

"Would you have believed me?"

Chantea did not believe her, of course. There were no such things as ghosts. The demons of her father's stories were echoes of the dark history of Earth. Omnia was empty, pristine, and safe.

"What did the ghost say?" she asked.

Maria pursed her lips. But it was Dave who spoke.

"What if there is something out there?"

Chantea lost her patience, never too strong to begin with. Between stories of ghosts and non-existent aliens, the Settlers' guilt was as clear to her as daylight. Still, there was the abduction of baby Eleni, the second missing child, which Dave and Maria could not have committed.

But other Settlers could.

Conspiracy!

Of course. What better way to create an alibi than to start with one of their own? Whether it was to strike at the Colonists, or more likely, to carry on the technos' abhorrent rituals, there was a Settler plot to abduct and kill babies! Chantea had no illusion that the abducted children were still alive. There was nowhere to hide them in the settlement, and two six-month-old babies could not survive on their own in the waste outside. But at least, she could prevent further deaths.

She motioned to one of her deputies to take the Hughes back to their cells. She was going to march to the Captain and demand the preventive incarceration of all the Settlers. Maria shuffled back, her head down, but Dave looked over his shoulder as he was led to his cell.

"There *is* something out there!" he said.

*   *   *

"No," Captain said.

"It's only twenty people!" Chantea protested. "Well, twenty-one."

She remembered the single Settler whose wife had died in the cryogenic chamber – a gloomy, prematurely aged, bearded man named Alexei Panov. Actually, thinking of this, he made a pretty good suspect – undoubtedly embittered by his loss and loneliness. Why hadn't she arrested him immediately?

"It does not matter how many," Nassrin replied. "Few of us are left, and we need everyone. We cannot sow more discord in the colony. Bring me proof."

Fuming, Chantea went back to her house which she shared with her daughter Akara and her niece Sophea.

Akara was home alone, watching some stupid Earthside vid on her tablet.

"Where is your cousin?" Chantea asked huffily.

"Went for a walk," Akara responded.

"What? Where?"

Akara gestured to the featureless plain plunged into the ochre dusk by the setting sun whose light faded into grey instead of blossoming into the bright colors of the Earth sunset.

"Why?"

Akara shrugged. "Just...something to see."

Chantea did not understand the point of taking a stroll in the dun wasteland, but her mind was still on the conspiracy and Captain's refusal to do something about it. She decided to bring it up before the Council next morning.

She and Akara shared an evening meal, and by the time she started worrying, the Small Moon had already streaked across the sky, briefly silvering the low range of eroded hills on the horizon like a broken crown.

Sophea did not come back.

20

*   *   *

Search parties found nothing on the plain. Tracking skills had been lost during the centuries in the cramped environs of the *Hope.* Captain ordered cameras installed around the perimeter of the town, but it was, as the ancient saying went, "locking the barn door after the horse was out". Akara was crying and upset, but the rest of the Colonists were enraged. A group of them attacked a Settler and beat him up.

Nassrin made a speech to the Council about peace and unity, which convinced nobody. She ordered Chantea to arrest anybody engaged in acts of violence, whether Settler of Colonist. Chantea listened to the order in surly silence but obeyed, conscripting more deputies and printing out more guns.

Chantea was organizing yet another search party when one of her deputies commed her with a report of a disturbance in the jail. Dave Hughes was hammering on his door, yelling to be let out to join the search for the missing children. Maria joined her husband from the adjoining cell.

Chantea's anger felt like a burning liquid rising in her gut, and she welcomed its acid sting. She hated the shivery helplessness of worry and despair. She marched to the jail and kicked open Dave's door.

He did not lunge at her, so she could not discharge her gun in self-defense as she had hoped. Instead, he poured out an excited stream of words, of which she understood barely half.

"What the fuck do you want?" she yelled. "Shut up, you baby-killer!"

Dave took a long breath and slowed down.

"I saw it," he said.

"You saw what?"

"The thing that took my son and the other children. Last night. In the dark. Flitting by the fence. I told you: there is something out there!"

"There is nothing out there," Chantea said contemptuously. "You should come up with a better story than that! Omnia is empty!"

21

"Why?"

"Why what?"

"Why is it empty? There is life in the sea. None on land."

Chantea shrugged. Science classes on the *Hope* were limited to the practical knowledge the Colonists would require in order to build their green paradise. Science had killed Earth. It would not be allowed to kill Omnia.

"It's a new planet," she said.

Dave snorted.

"New? Is that what you Colonists know? Gliese-18 is an old star, it's on its way to burning down into a red dwarf. Look outside; the rocks are eroded down to nothing. There are canyons, and gorges, and deep caves. There isn't much tectonic activity because the core is cooled. This planet should be crawling with life! Where is it?"

"Why are you telling me this?" Chantea demanded. "How do you know all of this anyway?"

Dave smiled crookedly.

"You think we are all bloodthirsty savages, don't you? Baby-killers. Do you know who built your bloody spaceship? People like me. We worked our butts off to give you a fighting chance, even though we knew you were being stupid. Generational ships don't work. But your ancestors were so determined to live close to nature on a pristine planet. So disgusted with science they blamed for the mess on Earth. And we did the impossible – built a slow spaceship that lasted for 300 years. And some of us went even further – put ourselves into deep freeze, knowing we only had twenty percent chance of coming out alive or with our brains not turned to mush. Maria and I… we left our home. We left our families. We took a gamble. And you are telling me we murdered our son?"

"Why?" Chantea asked, impressed despite herself. "Why did you do it? Went into a cryogenic chamber?"

"Because we are exobiologists, both of us. You didn't know it, did you? You probably don't even know what it means. But we gave up everything for the chance to study alien life up close. To touch it, smell it, hell, maybe even to communicate with it. And I am telling you: there is life on this planet, no matter what your dumb probes show. And this life is responsible for what happened to Andrew and the others. Let me go onto the plain. I will find my son."

*　　*　　*

Dave left at dawn, equipped with a drone camera and a primitive comm that only worked at line-of-sight. Much of the tech on the *Hope* got damaged in the Blackout, so they had nothing more sophisticated to give him. He wanted to have a gun; Chantea initially refused but Nassrin ordered a new gun printed out that she could disable remotely. Chantea, however, had her way in not letting Maria join her husband, despite his argument that she was a better biologist than he. She had been the one to suggest they check out the range of rocky hills riven with gorges and caves, about five kilometers from the town. If there was life on Omnia, it was hiding from sight; and what better place to hide than subterranean caverns?

He had to walk rather than ride in a crawler because the entire desperate operation was hush-hush. A rebellion against Captain's lenient treatment of the Settlers was brewing; and the news that the man suspected of killing his own son was let out of jail would precipitate an explosion.

Every ten minutes, Dave reported back, and his drone sent a burst of pictures. They showed the same thing Chantea saw every time she looked beyond the green of the fields: the bare ochre ground, occasionally streaked with the dark brown of some mineral deposit; the gleaming ribbon of a creek; the dull reddish glow of the sun filtered through the thin clouds.

"No tracks," Dave said. "But the ground is firm. They may be careful not to leave traces."

"Your mysterious aliens?" Chantea scoffed.

The comm suddenly filled with ear-splitting noise. The visual feed broke up, and when it came back, it showed Dave standing in front of a sandstone formation eroded into jutting spires like broken teeth. A low yellow

23

cliff loomed beyond it. And gaping in the cliff wall was a black hole. A cavemouth, big enough for a man to walk through.

Dave flashlight flickered off glassy stalactites as he scrambled down the incline of the cave's floor. The drone hovered above him, sending vids of the petrified waterfall of flowstone and of the deposit-encrusted walls.

And then the feed was cut off.

Chantea swore.

"I told you, he would try to escape!" she yelled.

"Escape where?" Nassrin asked evenly. "Nobody can survive on Omnia alone. They would starve."

"There are squigglies," Chantea retorted, but she knew it was nonsense. Nobody had ever tried eating the tiny aquatic organisms.

"I understand you are concerned about your niece," Nassrin said, "but you need to be objective. You represent the law, Chantea. Without the law, we are no better than animals."

"I *am* objective," Chantea said. "And logical. This charade about hidden life...the probes would have found it. It does not exist. My niece and the rest of the children were killed by the Settlers."

"I read about Earth history," Nassrin said. "Baby-killing. That was the most common accusation against despised and persecuted groups. And it always led to bloodshed. I am not going to let it happen on Omnia."

"And maybe some of these accusations were true," Chantea muttered, but did not openly challenge Nassrin. She was Captain.

For now.

They waited; Chantea ruminating over her next steps. The fate of her niece was, contrary to what Nassrin implied, not foremost in her mind. She did not like Sophea. Nor had she liked her sister, Sophea's mum, who had died in the Blackout together with her husband. The Blackout had been so traumatic that Chantea has asked Aker Jonasson for medication to blunt her memory of it. She did not want to relive the humiliation of helplessness and fear as she flailed in the thick darkness, waiting for the aging bots to restore gravity and light. Sophea was an unwitting reminder of that humiliation. Chantea had taken her in as a matter of familial obligation and because it would enhance her unsuccessful run for Captain.

The dusk had fallen; and still there was nothing on the screen. Until suddenly, there was.

The drone floated back from the cavemouth and started uploading its entire stock of images taken inside. At the same time, the display on the side of the screen showed quick pings. Dave was firing his sidearm inside the cave.

"Stop it!" Chantea demanded. Nassrin could remotely jam the gun's mechanism. But she shook her head.

The shots stopped, but the images continued uploading. Nassrin took a deep breath, Chantea bit her lip.

"Bring Maria in!" Captain commanded.

The Settler woman sat heavily some distance away from Captain and Sheriff.

The quality of the vid was appalling. Dave's flashlight produced a tangle of dancing shadows, among which his own silhouette loomed like a deformed giant. The drone was malfunctioning, tilting and lurching, taking random shots of the walls and the ceiling. It was clear, though, that the cave was much deeper than expected: a tunnel rather than a hole in the rocks.

"Wait!" Maria paused the display at a murky shot of the tunnel's wall.

"What?" Chantea barked.

Maria pointed to something – a recessed oval, slightly darker than the sandstone, surrounded by a halo of thin lines.

"It's a fossil," she said. "A big one. Something like a trilobite."

Chantea tried to remember what a fossil was, but Captain was quicker.

"Life," she said.

Maria smiled crookedly, showing her large white teeth.

"Yes," she said. "Real life. Not squigglies."

"But the probes found nothing."

"Because they were not looking in the right places."

On screen, Dave, followed by the drone, was walking deeper underground, the tunnel dipping down, becoming almost a ramp, smooth, as if polished by water. Chantea had to remind herself that this was not a real-time transmission. This was the past. The drone was out but Dave was still inside, and his gun was not firing anymore.

Dave stopped at the entrance to a larger cavern. The beam of his flashlight disappearing in the darkness.

The picture glitched, then stabilized. A face was looking back at them.

Perhaps "looking" was a wrong word. It had no eyes.

A white oval, as delicate as porcelain, glabrous and smooth. A tiny rosebud mouth, a straight nose. A fringe of bleached hair. And two shallow indentations like thumbprints in wet clay under its blonde eyebrows.

"What the hell?" Chantea heard herself say, and even normally self-contained Nassrin made a strangled sound. Maria jumped to her feet, her chair cluttering to the side, as she bent closely to the screen.

The face was not alone. Several more appeared. They clustered at the far wall of the cavern. The drone hung by the ceiling, so the figures to which the faces were attached appeared weirdly foreshortened. They were small and shapeless, clad in billowing robes that covered their bodies apart from the paper-white eyeless masks of their faces.

One of the figures moved, an arm snaking out from beneath its robe, holding something...and the screen went black. Chantea blinked, trying to resolve the fleeting image of something terribly wrong about the creature's hand.

"His light has gone out," Nassrin said.

"They broke it," Maria said.

"A projectile?"

"Their hands are like a frog's legs – with adhesive pads."

The drone kept on recording, but they could not see anything.

"Why doesn't it have a flash?" Nassrin demanded. The answer was that nobody had thought of adding it. Recording technology was not held in high regard in the colony because it did not contribute to their pastoral survival.

Chantea studied the grainy blackness of the vid. There was some movement in the smears of shadows.

"Can we enhance it?" she asked. Nassrin was already tinkering with the display, and the last picture brightened up, turning into a chiaroscuro of shades of gray.

Dave was on his knees on the floor of the cavern, surrounded by the eyeless creatures who clung to him like kids taking a ride on their father's shoulders. But no father ever had to carry so many; and no kids ever plummeted upon their father from above, spreading their robes like wings and swooping through the air. A couple of them hung from the ceiling. Chantea remembered the natural history vids of Earth bats she had seen in school.

And then the feed blinked out altogether. When it came back on, the drone was transmitting from outside the township, hobbling on the hardpan like a wounded rabbit. Dave was nowhere in sight.

There was a long silence and then Captain turned to the two women.

"I'm sorry for your loss," she said to Maria. And then, addressing Chantea: "Now you see. There *are* aliens here. The Settlers are not to blame."

"These are no aliens," Maria said.

Both Nassrin and Chantea stared at her. Her face was stony, showing no emotions.

"What do you mean?" Chantea hissed. "Didn't you and your husband get frozen in order to see alien life? Well, here it is!"

Maria did not look back at her.

"Yes," she said, "Dave and I are...were ... exobiologists. And yes, that was what we wanted. What we lived for. We saw data brought in by FTL probes and realized just how alien life on other planets is. We tried to study it. But nobody was interested. Earth was dying, and pure science was not on anybody's list of priorities. Your ancestors just wanted to get the hell out of climate change and political instability. They were not explorers or even pioneers. They were refugees."

Chantea opened her mouth to protest, but Nassrin silenced her with a look.

"I understand,' she said. "Maybe better than you know. But now we saw that aliens exist. You can study them. I'm sorry about your family, but this is what you wanted, isn't it? And we need to understand what they are if we are to survive on what we thought was an empty planet."

Maria shook her head.

"I told you," she said, "when we looked at the data, we saw planets with carbon-based biospheres. But there was nothing that even remotely resembled Earth life-forms. All those dreams of a parallel evolution...steamy planets with dinosaur lookalikes...it is nonsense. Anthropocentric dreams. We could not even tell plants from animals, or intelligent life from natural processes. So how are these creatures so humanlike?"

"Humanlike?" Chantea scoffed. "They have no eyes!"

"Most cave-dwelling organisms on Earth lose their eyesight. You don't need it in perpetual darkness. But other than that...they have two legs, two arms, a nose and a mouth. They are not alien enough to *be* aliens."

"So, what are they?" Nassrin asked.

"I don't know. But they are the ones who took my son and the other children."

"What do you think they did with them?"

Maria shrugged. "Ate them? Adopted them? How should I know?" She got up and went to the door, throwing over her shoulder. "I'm going home. Unless you want to put me back in jail."

Chantea stirred, but Nassrin forestalled her and motioned for the woman to go away. After that, Chantea exploded.

"Did you hear that? 'Ate them?' How could she be so...callous? I'm telling you: the Settlers are not human!"

"The Settlers are human," Nassrin said tiredly. "But the more pressing question is: what are these cave creatures?"

Chantea bit her lip. The evidence of the drone feed was irrefutable. Unless...couldn't Dave somehow have faked it? The Settlers had technological skills, learned on old Earth, that the Colonists did not possess. What better way to divert suspicion from himself than shift it to nonexistent aliens?

She explained her theory to Captain who was skeptical. But she agreed with Chantea's suggestion not to disclose the vid to the Colonists until more evidence could be collected. By the time it was done, the vid was irrelevant anyway.

*   *   *

Next day, two events occurred which put an end to Chantea's plan to send an armed group of deputies into the caves. First was the death of Alexei Panov, the solitary Settler. He was found in his tiny home dead, his face beaten into bloody pulp.

The second event was something Chantea did not know at the time. Only the Captain and a group of workers from the agricultural district were aware of what was happening. The supervisor of the district made his panicky report to Nassrin, and she instantly put a gag order on the information. It delayed chaos for all of three hours.

Meanwhile, Chantea was busy with investigating the crime scene of Panov's murder. Not that it required any outstanding detective skills. Pinned to the victim's chest was a piece of paper with crudely scrawled words *Baby-killer.*

Now Chantea was fully justified in her decision to put all the Settlers under arrest for their own protection – so much so that she did not consult Nassrin before sending her deputies to round them up and lock them in the Assembly Hall, temporarily used as a detention center.

They did not go quietly. By the time it was done, two Settlers were dead, and a deputy wounded.

Chantea walked into the Assembly Hall, her gun conspicuously on the ready. She spotted Maria immediately. She was wiping the blood off a man's face but got to her feet when Chantea beckoned to her.

"So, you are beginning to kill us off," she said.

"You may be sure that Panov's killer will be apprehended and punished," Chantea responded. "I'm the Sheriff, and nobody takes the law in their own hands on my watch."

"The law? Really, Sheriff? So, do you still believe that we kill children, including our own? After what we have seen in the cave?"

Chantea hesitated. She clung to her theory of a fake, but after a sleepless night, she still could not come up with any satisfactory explanation as how it could have been done. Settlers did not have access to such technology. She doubted anybody in the township did.

"If those creatures are not aliens, what are they?" she asked. "Come on, you must have some theory. You are a scientist, right?"

She hoped the word "scientist", encrusted as it was with layers of fear and contempt, sounded neutral on her lips.

Maria stepped toward the window, away from her fellow Settlers, and turned to Chantea. "Judging by what I saw," she said carefully, "I'd say they were human beings adapted to cave-dwelling."

"But this is impossible! We are the first humans on Omnia!"

"As far as we know."

"Are you saying that there had been another generational ship before the Hope?"

Maria shook her head.

"I don't know anything about it, and I doubt it would have been possible. But what about...?"

There was a plopping sound, followed by a shuttered glass, and Maria slumped onto the floor. Chantea was blinded by a spray of warm liquid into her eyes. It took her a couple of heartbeats to realize it was blood.

*   *   *

Chantea staggered into Captain's quarters, wiping sweat and dust off her face. Nassrin sat at the screen, staring at the live feed from the settlement.

Chantea and her recently drafted deputies were outnumbered by the rampaging mob of Colonists. Despite Nassrin's order to use live ammunition to protect the remaining Settlers, the Assembly Hall was overrun. Colonists, brandishing illegally printed guns, knives and household tools, broke inside. When Captain arrived at the scene, trying to calm down the mob, she was rudely pushed aside, and Chantea only just managed to whisk her to safety. When the deputies finally prevailed, all but three Settlers were dead.

Now those three, two men and a woman, sat on the floor in Nassrin's quarters, their eyes glazed with shock. Aker Jonasson, their doctor, was administering sedatives and analgesics.

Outside, the settlement looked like one of the cautionary vids from the last days of Earth Chantea had seen in school. Group of people, disheveled, covered in dust and the blood of their neighbors, roamed the streets. The prefab homes where Settlers used to live were set on fire. Captain had turned down the sound but the chants of "Death to baby-killers" were still audible. And above all of it, the dim sky of Omnia was getting dimmer, as its tired sun was crawling toward the horizon, and the night of the Small Moon was coming.

Nassrin turned to Chantea, and of all the horrors of this horrible day, it was Captain's face that shocked her most. Nassrin had been elected Captain after the Blackout because of her unshakeable calm and soothing wisdom. The Colonists, spooked like the children left alone in the dark, had needed a maternal presence to soothe them. But now she looked as sharp as a hatchet, her narrow features set in a mask of unrelenting determination. Chantea remembered that Captain's ancestors had been warriors.

31

"I am going into the cave," she said.

"What? No! These creatures...monsters..."

"Monsters? And what are we?"

Chantea looked away from the screen.

"They will calm down," she said.

"No. Not when they learn that there is no food left. If you think prejudice alone is destructive, try prejudice *and* famine."

"No food left?" Chantea repeated, her brain curling up like a wounded hedgehog. "How?"

Nassrin shifted the display, and Chantea saw the agricultural district. The fields, recently overabundant with fast-growing crops, were a wasteland of charred sticks and black sludge. Greenhouses were filled with liquid rot. Fruit trees were gray skeletons. And when the drone cameras panned to the rabbit hatches and chicken runs, she saw pitiful bodies of small animals and birds heaped up in the indiscriminate abandon of death.

"How?" she whispered with numbed lips.

"It is the sun," said one of the Settlers, an older man with gray hair and a haggard face. Chantea did not remember his name.

"What do you mean, the sun?"

"I was an astronomer," the man said. "On Earth. Before astronomy was defunded as a frivolous pursuit, not contributing to preservation of nature and fight against climate change. Anyway, I studied the data on Gliese-18, and there was something funny about the spectrum. I did not know what it was, and I tried to warn the founders of Project Hope but of course, nobody would listen. They saw an empty planet, perfectly suitable for 32ecreateng the earthly paradise that they imagined. But I was curious. So, I volunteered to be frozen. I knew my chances, but there was nothing left on Earth for me anyway. So...I guess I was lucky. I am here, right?"

"What was it about the spectrum?" Nassrin demanded.

"This star emits a lot of ultraviolet radiation, very unusual for a yellow dwarf. UV is deadly to life unless filtered by the ozone layer. But the ozone layer is not formed here because, even though Omnia has oxygen, it is so old that it lacks a magnetic field, and so radiation breaks up ozone molecules. UV is so harsh here that it basically sterilizes the surface."

"This is why the planet is empty," Chantea said slowly, her mind trying to wrap itself around ideas that went against everything she had ever been taught and used to believe. "It's empty because it kills life."

"Right," Nassrin said. "And now it is killing us."

"This amount of UV," the Settler man said, "can also cause brain tumors and neurological disorders. I wouldn't be surprised if those...murderers out there are not in their right minds. If they ever were."

Nassrin got up, and Chantea saw that her peaceful Captain had two newly printed guns tucked into her belt.

"I am going to the caves," she said tonelessly. "And I am going to shoot every rioter who crosses my path. Chantea, you are the acting Captain. Stop the riot. Arrest everybody you can lay your hands on. We will have trials when I come back. Everyone who killed a Settler will be executed on the spot."

"But this is..." Chantea started.

"Barbaric? No, this is justice."

"But why are you going?"

"Because these people are our only hope. They have survived here for centuries. They can teach us how."

"What centuries?" And then Chantea saw it.

"FTL drive," she whispered. "It was perfected after the Hope departed."

"Yes. They came here 300 years before our planetfall. And their descendants still live here."

"Descendants? They are not human!"

The eyeless porcelain-white masks, the spread-out cloaks like batwings, small bodies clinging to the cave-walls...

"Maybe being human is not all it is cracked out to be," Nassrin replied.

Chantea watched Captain step outside. She was quickly engulfed by the rampaging mob. Chantea heard the sharp crack of a shot and then silence.

The lurid glare of the burning prefabs was the only illumination outside, as the sun had set, and the dull dusk was curdling into the night. On the outskirts of the mob, small figures flitted in the gathering darkness, firelight gleaming on their porcelain faces.

Chantea pulled out her gun.

"I am Captain now," she declared to the huddle of her disoriented deputies. "We are going to defend ourselves. We are going to defend humanity."

She walked to the door but before exiting, she turned around and shot the Settler astronomer through the head.

Here Be Monsters
K. S. Hardy

In hand-lettered script
Often in Latin or Greek
Reads the legend
On some blank corner
Of the parchment map
With a sea serpent
Crafted from the illustrator's
Fear-fired imagination

On a similar star map
In the A. I.'s memory
The words also appear
Touching the third world
From a small star
And near it the drawing
Of a bipedal creature
To be avoided at all costs.

What We Leave Behind
MM Schreier

The air in my EVA suit tastes tinny. Can O2 canisters go bad? It's not that I have a choice—breathe the metal-flavored air or open my helmet and let a cocktail of poison gases fill my lungs.

I sigh. We had high hopes for this little rocky terrestrial planet. The grav's higher than I'm used to, so I shuffle my boots instead of picking up my feet and taking proper steps. Angry clouds of rust-colored dust billow in my wake, like miniature tempests. Everything's angry here, but it's not the lack of atmosphere that makes the planet uninhabitable. It's the damned soil.

If we can't grow oxygen-generating plants, the whole project's worthless.

I wind my way through the PDBs—planetary design bots. They're useless here. Gears and tracks are shrouded in red dust, the sugar-fine particles worming their way in to short out electronics and blanket sensors. Even the self-cleaning nanobot protocols can't keep up.

An hour ago, I sent my final report to HQ.

Planetary designation Alpha Niner Charlie Zero Tri Victor unsuitable for terraforming. Breaking camp to return to The Pathfinder. ETA to next prospective site: six rotations.

At the time, I was disappointed I wouldn't get my bonus. Not to mention half a revolution in cryo to look forward to. Seems unimportant now.

The wind whipped up the ever-present dust, and heat lightning streaked across a darkening sky.

"Portia! Hurry up! The launch window's closing." Tailian's voice crackled through the comms at an unnaturally high frequency. One could almost call it shrill. But that was all wrong, Taili was the definition of self-control.

"I'll be right behind you in Jumper Two. Rendezvous at The Pathfinder in three minutes. I just need to prep the PBDs." It was bad enough this god-forsaken rock cost us our bonuses, but we'd be docked a rotation's pay if the terraforming equipment got damaged.

"Roger that."

The view beyond my EVA helmet dimmed as Jumper One's thruster engaged and tossed even more dust around. For a moment, I stood lost in the swirling plumes. The crimson and orange puffs looked like striped mounds of cotton candy. I grinned, sending the thought to my remote memory storage. There was a poem in there somewhere.

A flash lit the dust cloud, and then a wave of fire knocked me off my feet.

I shake off the memory but can't help but glance over my shoulder at the Jumpers' wreckage. Damned lightning. I should have convinced Tailian to wait out the storm, but I had wanted off planet just as much as she did. We'd dreamed of real showers and food replicators after countless cycles of EVA sanitation and dehydrated meal pouches.

My stomach grumbles. What I wouldn't give for just one more taste of freeze-dried pad thai. I could almost feel the odd crunch of desiccated vegetables between my teeth and—

Elevation 3,000 meters.

The text across my visor interrupts my food daydream. My feet no longer kick up dust devils as the ground shifts from its blanket of fine-grained particles to bare, black-and-red striated rock. Ahead, an isolated stone shelf reaches upward.

With nothing better to do, I climb.

My calves burn, but the view's spectacular. From this height, I can see endless clicks in every direction. Roving storms waltz across the valley, women with swirling iron-dust ballgowns and lightning woven in their hair.

More poetic images for memory upload.

Base camp is a toy village the giant dancers have stomped on, unaware of what they crushed beneath their feet.

My heart constricts as I suck in the damned tinny air. Taili's ragdoll body is lost in the rubble. Torn apart. Incinerated. Ashy bone flecks mingling with the dust. Perhaps it's for the best, for the rescuers. No, not rescuers, the recovery team. The nearest ship is eleven years out. Better there's nothing left of Taili to find. I, on the other hand, will be something for them to talk about with their therapists—a mummified corpse in an EVA suit.

I shudder. That image doesn't get stored.

At the top of the stone shelf, I sit and dangle my feet over the edge.

Air reserves critical.

I turn off the overlays. Better to belay the inevitable updates.

Below, magma boils from a crack in the ground. These little pockets of molten rock aren't unusual. A9C03V seems irritable with its electrical storms, choking dust, and rivers of lava. Perhaps it has a right to be mad. After all, we showed up unannounced with plans to change its face to build spas and casinos for the rich to throw credits away on a whim.

I don't store that thought either.

Instead, I think of Tailian's smile—how white her teeth were against her dark skin. The way she'd laugh like a drunk hyena when she caught me singing in the shower. How she always made sure the ship mind roused her first from cryo, so she could be the first thing I saw when I woke.

The ground rumbles and bits of stone break free from the shelf, cascading down the cliff face. My spine rattles as the earthquake shakes my seat. Magma spits and sparks fly into the air. They flicker like overgrown fireflies showing off for their mates.

Flash. Blink. Fade.

A second quake thunders and a crevice forms in the rock. I pay it no mind, unable to tear my eyes from the capering fireflies. The air in my suit no longer tastes tinny. It's like summer—saltwater taffy and the scent of wildflowers. Warmth that radiates on skin, even after sunset. Fireflies dancing for the ones they love.

There are only seconds to upload the images before the shelf breaks free.

In that moment I'm not falling, I soar with the spark-flies. Together, we dive toward the crimson light below.

Maybe the recovery team won't need to talk to their therapists about me after all.

Smiling, I upload one last glorious thought to leave behind.

Flight.

Zarmina

Lisa Short

Gliese 581g ("Zarmina"), Terraform Monitoring Station Alpha: 2181-02-04-1900

Tensions had been running high aboard the *Mary Jackson* when Auris Delleray left it; she'd almost been relieved to shuttle down to Gliese 581g. Though her anticipated solitude, once she'd reached the planetary surface, hadn't actually equated to *silence*—too many of the rest of the *Mary's* crew had already found out the hard way that they couldn't stand it, the incessant screaming of the storms that beat against the surface stations' outer hulls. But Auris preferred the storms to the sorts of conversations that had been breaking up the far more sullen silences to be found aboard the *Mary* these days.

Auris was listening to the latest storm now, a real doozy, from the dubious comfort of Station Alpha's Hub. The storm had slammed into the station ten hours earlier and still showed no signs of letting up; Auris thought the storms in general might be worsening, or at least increasing in duration, as the terraforming-driven volcanic activity intensified. She leaned back in her chair at the Hub's main console, eyes closing—she was rather tired; this particular storm had blown in just as she'd been turning in the night before and had awoken her more than once.

A sharp, thin beep jerked her eyes back open, startling her with the realization that she had actually started to doze off, *on duty!*—she hastily checked the console display. The audible alert had been the station's surface-to-orbital communications array losing contact with the *Mary*, a not-infrequent event during a storm. A quick query to the console brought back a schematic of the three other monitoring stations on Gliese 581g, one for each major planetary landmass, all shining the cool blue of open comm channels. And as a matter of fact, it *was* time, a bit past really, to check in with Station Charlie five thousand kilometers to the north.

Auris tapped Station Charlie's icon on the console display. A minute later, a cheery voice echoed through the emptiness of Station Alpha's Hub: "Zarmina Station Charlie, all's well! Hey, is that Auris?"

"Hi, Casey." Auris found herself smiling involuntarily; Casey had that effect on nearly everyone, even through an audio-only channel. "When did you get down here? I thought you weren't scheduled for planetside duty for another month."

"I wasn't." Casey sounded glum. "But Danni decided he just couldn't come back down again. He lost comms to the ship for an entire week, his last rotation—he had a genuine panic attack right there in the *Mary's* shuttle bay when yesterday's launch window opened. So here I am." She sighed. "It's almost a third of the crew now that can't come down for planetside duty—Dr. Micale thinks we've got more on our hands than just *good old-fashioned cabin fever.*" Auris grinned at that; Casey had an eerily good knack for imitating voices, good enough that Auris could almost hear Dr. Micale's precise, measured cadences in her own head. "He told me he thinks the sheer length of the trip out here, in an entirely closed space surrounded by an utterly hostile environment—he thinks that a lot of people are coping with that by developing roaring cases of agoraphobia."

"Agoraphobia, huh?" Auris rubbed her forehead; a tension headache was starting up right between her eyebrows. "Weren't we all screened for that before we left Earth?"

"The good doctor says this is a really specific kind of agoraphobia, it wouldn't necessarily show up during a standard psych eval. Basically, their subconscious minds have decided that only the *Mary* is safe, and the trauma of losing ship comms on top of that—"

"Speaking of which, this is *my* official notification that I've lost comms with the ship—you might want to check your board too, if you've had a storm recently."

"Hmm, give me a sec. Well, shit. Same here, no ship comms." A brief pause. "Not much of a loss, though, really. Not the way people have been acting lately." Casey's voice tensed. "Uh, *you're* a NorAm citizen, right?" The next pause was noticeably longer. "Um—"

Auris decided to stop messing with her. "Yeah. But I don't care. I *really* don't—I wasn't paying attention to the news even before we left Earth. I'm sorry there's fighting, of course, but if it ends quicker by SouAm swallowing up half of NorAm, I'm totally fine with that. Honestly."

Casey exhaled loudly into the mic. "Well, I wish everyone else felt that way—I don't care about the whole NorAm-SouAm thing either, but I can't usually say so because then they're all like oh of *course* you don't care, you're *not even from The West*—"

Auris snickered. "Wait, let me guess. Was that Kimber?" Kimber Alencon was not only a NorAm citizen, but also hailed from NorAm's Dakota enclave, where they tended to consider most other geopolitical groupings of humanity as lustful, raging hordes slavering away at NorAm's borders. They regarded the proposed secession of the entire lower third of NorAm, especially the parts left over from the old United States, into the SouAm Confederación to be nothing short of sacrilege.

"Yup. Couldn't you hear *The Capital Letters?*"

After a few more exchanges of a purely social nature, Auris and Casey moved on to the official communication checklist—*are all the automated landers communicating, did the latest seismic and geothermal data upload to the* Mary, *did you see that shift in weather patterns at the equator?*— then signed off.

Less than an hour later, with startling abruptness, the howling of the storm outside died down to a low moan. Auris instructed the Hub console to lower the viewport shields, then trotted over to the main viewport. Her ears had not deceived her; the storm had gone. The endless twilight of Gliese 581g's current sky was on full display, wispy with clouds; she liked the view, at least when it wasn't storming, in spite of its undeniable desolation. 581g's weather system had been mostly nonexistent before the automated terraforming landers had touched down forty years ago; the mountains in the distance had only suffered through a few decades of erosion since and were still as sharp as cut black glass against the violet horizon.

Thinking she might as well try to catch up on her sleep now that it was quiet outside, Auris ambled off toward the crew cabin, glancing over her shoulder at the main viewport for one last look at the scenery.

A face! A face in the viewport! A FACE!

Auris jerked backward, lost her balance, and staggered sideways in a fruitless attempt to regain it before she thumped down onto the floor. She lost sight of the face on the way down, *the face!*—she scrambled frantically back up onto her feet, barking her shin hard against the Hub's main console.

But the face was gone.

If you even saw a face—

Hadn't she? A man's face—bearded, heavy-browed, the features distorted through a pressure suit's faceplate, the suit the dirty off-white of the *Mary's* standard issue.

Or just a shadow from a passing cloud? Or just the way the light hit the window at that particular moment? Or—

Maybe she hadn't seen anything. Of *course* she hadn't seen anything!—no one would be standing outside the station's main viewport staring *in* at her. And certainly not a face she didn't recognize—after the full two shipboard years it had taken the crew of the *Mary* to travel from Sol to Gliese 581, they had all gotten to know each other far better than they might ever have wanted. Blurred or not, she knew every single face that could show up on 581g for literally millions of kilometers in every direction. Auris shook herself irritably and limped off toward Station Alpha's tiny crew cabin.

Gliese 581g ("Zarmina"), Terraform Monitoring Station Alpha: 2181-02-05-0800

Auris had trouble sleeping. Without the storm to drown them out, the nearly inaudible creaks and groans of the station's support struts settling kept shooting little jolts of adrenaline through her. She couldn't remember those sounds bothering her before on her previous two duty rotations, but after an hour of trying to argue herself out of noticing them at all, she gave up and groped for the tiny personal console next to her bunk. But piping music from the Hub's archives over the station's speakers somehow made it even worse; the acoustics in the Hub rendered the music tinny, unreal, oddly spiteful.

She finally managed to fall into a restless doze a few hours before the on-duty alert was set to go off; she felt like she'd just barely closed her eyes when its sharp, annoying buzz jerked her awake once more. She fumbled her station coveralls back on and staggered back out of the cabin, rubbing her forehead where the tension headache had apparently settled in for the long haul. The tiny crew cabin opened directly out into the Hub—most of the station *was* the Hub, except for the cabin, the half-walled kitchenette nook directly opposite it, and the airlocks. Auris settled down once more in front of the main console and made herself go through the start-of-shift checklist. Communications with the *Mary* were still out, even though the storm had been over for hours—she supposed that the comm array's self-repair bots must have encountered unusually bad storm damage.

Then Station Charlie's icon pulsed yellow, right under her reaching fingers; Auris blinked down at it. Charlie wasn't scheduled for another Station Alpha check-in for two days. Dubiously, Auris jabbed at the icon.

"Can you believe it, oh my *God!*" Casey's voice crackled over the comm.

"Uh—Zarmina Station Alpha, all's well—

"*Fine,* all's well here too, but can you be *lieve* it?"

"Believe what?"

"Seriously? Wait—haven't you talked to the ship yet?"

"No, my array's still down—"

"There's a *ship,* another ship, *in-system!*"

Auris stared blankly down at the console. "What? Where?"

"Not all that close—I mean, they *are* in-system, but still about twenty light-minutes out from 581g's orbit."

"Twenty light-minutes? But they're just now communicating with us?"

"Uh, yeah. I guess—"

"Did they say why they hadn't hailed us before?"

"I...guess not? I don't know, I didn't actually talk to them myself." Casey's tone brightened again. "It's a Coalition ship, if you can believe that!" Auris was silent. "Wow, Auris, you really meant it when you said you didn't follow the news. You *do* know about the Coalition, right?"

"I know what the Coalition is," said Auris slowly. "I just didn't know they had spaceships."

"Well, apparently they do, and they're here to assess if it's possible to start colonization a little early—"

"A *little* early?"

"Like, by the end of the century."

"Do they know that 581g's not going to have surface oxygen concentrations higher than five percent for at least another fifty years? Not to mention livable surface temps, and the storms—"

"They want to build the first colony underground and use heat pumps and oxygen concentrators, or something like that—look, I'm a biologist, not a facilities specialist." Casey's tone had taken on an edge. "We can use all the help we can get on this project, right? With so many of us barred from groundside duty at this point. And anyway, the Coalition is *cool.*"

So they tell everyone who'll listen, Auris thought, but didn't say aloud. She made a concerted effort to regain the cordiality of the previous day's comms with Casey, but wasn't sure if she had succeeded by the time they ended the session. Maybe she was still just tense from the night before—after whatever it was she'd seen...just *seeing something* wasn't so bad, didn't mean she was going off the deep end or anything. People did that all the time, tried to fit some random shape glimpsed for a split-second to a template of all the stored memories in their heads— there was nothing wrong with her. Nothing.

Though maybe she should stop by and speak to Dr. Micale herself, once she was back aboard the *Mary.* Just to be sure.

Auris dutifully placed check-in calls to Stations Bravo and Delta at the appointed times. Medea Paellas at Bravo wanted to ramble on endlessly on the subject of the incoming arrivals to the Gliese 581 system, much as Casey had; apparently, Auris was the only one who still didn't have ship comms restored. And Delta didn't answer at all—Auris double-checked the console display, but Delta's icon still shone uninterrupted blue. The protocol for terraforming station personnel failing to check in when there were no obvious technological problems was to inform the ship—of *course* it was. Annoyed, Auris decided to suit up, go outside and take a look at Station Alpha's array herself. She was no expert at it, but she should at least be able to tell what stage of self-repair it was at; if it still seemed hours away from operability, she'd call up Casey to comm the *Mary* for her.

The suit locker was right next to the groundside airlock. The station had a second airlock built into its roof, for shuttle transfers, but she had stowed her suit in the hatch beside the groundside lock after she'd disembarked for just this sort of eventuality. She popped the locker open and started dragging her pressure suit out, then stopped, frowning. The suit's tough outer skin was oddly slick under her fingers—*damp?* And she'd done a terrible job packing it away—it almost looked as if she'd just haphazardly shoved it in there, rather than carefully bundling it up into the approved folds. She tried to remember actually packing it into the locker, but had no more than the most abstract memory of doing so— obviously she *had* done it, as it was there, but she'd clearly paid no heed to the process at the time. How could it still be *damp*, though...? Station Alpha's internal air was dry enough that any moisture should have evaporated off it within a few hours of stowage...shouldn't it?

So, well, obviously it hadn't—she sighed, then dragged the suit the rest of the way out of the locker and began the laborious process of struggling into it. Ten minutes later, she was finally outside the station, standing on open ground that was not on Earth for only the sixth time in her life.

Auris paused at the outer threshold of the exterior airlock door, briefly caught by the wonder of it all in spite of her tiredness. The sky arched infinitely far overhead, still mysterious twilight and studded with hazy stars; Gliese 581's day lasted nearly as long as its year did. Dull gray rock, ranging from pebble-sized to rivalling Station Alpha itself in height and breadth, peppered the icy, reddish-black dirt stretching out to the distant mountains. *Another world*—gazing out at that alien landscape, its newness and sheer potential, soothed her raw nerves enough that she set off for the comm array in slightly better spirits.

The array itself was just a few hundred meters from the station, hidden behind one of the larger rock formations in the hopes that putting it there would mitigate some of the inevitable storm damage. It wasn't a fun slog, in the heavy, clumsy pressure suit—Auris's thoughts began wandering again as she lumbered across the frozen terrain.

The Coalition—they were aggressively nonnational, a status that gave them a lot of leeway in terms of people's knee-jerk reaction to them. They did openly eschew all the old, rigid racial and gender theories that still had so many stubborn adherents on Earth, embracing all persons and cultures from a foundation of strict egalitarianism—a pinnacle of both logical and moral authority, right?

Except that nobody knew quite who they were. Who their popular spokespeople were, yes—but their executive staff and top-level administrators? No. The Coalition claimed that they had received so many credible death threats from various quasi-to-outright terrorist groups that they had to stay anonymous. A reasonable assertion, certainly—no one could deny that—but...a spaceship? *Colonies?* Auris racked her brain for any scrap of anything like that she'd ever seen in any news release about the Coalition—and admittedly, she never paid much attention to any news releases of a political nature, but surely she'd have noticed something like that—

Auris reached the array's rock formation not a moment too soon; the eastern horizon had started to blur ominously, probably with an incoming storm. She shuffled laboriously around the formation, then stopped in astonishment at the sight of what had clearly once been the comm array and now was nothing more than several square meters of shattered metal, glass and plastic. The *entire* comm array had been wrecked—by the last storm? Had that ever happened before? No wonder it hadn't fixed itself yet—its self-repair bots were probably buried somewhere underneath all that mess, possibly nothing more than shattered pieces themselves. Auris tore her gaze away from the destroyed array long enough to spare the approaching storm a nervous glance, then turned her back on it and started moving as fast as she could back toward the station.

Auris cycled back though the station airlock as quickly as its automatics would allow, then struggled out of the pressure suit, kicking it to one side as she hurried over to the Hub's main console. Her fingers were already reaching for Station Charlie's icon when she realized it was blinking bright, merciless red—and not only it, but every single other station icon as well. She stared blankly down at the console. The stations didn't use the main array outside to talk to each other; they used the comm network built into the automated terraforming landers. She'd lost communication with *all* the other stations? Just now? The silence of the Hub, usually soothing, seemed to press down on her like a physical force.

And then she heard it—a sound. A *thump*, a *scrape* —she wasn't sure which, except that it was coming from inside the hub. *Inside—!* Auris looked around wildly, but the Hub was empty—of course it was empty. The inset ceiling lights had dimmed to the sleep shift setting while she was gone, but even what shadows there were, behind the kitchenette half-wall and under the comm console itself, were too diffuse to hide anything. Or anybody.

The storm hit the outside of the station with a muffled howl of wrath. Auris flinched reflexively, head jerking with the motion—then her gaze snagged on the crew cabin door. It was closed. Had she closed it earlier, after she'd left the cabin? She usually didn't bother. She couldn't remember closing it—she couldn't remember *not* closing it, either. *If someone came in here, while I was out at the array*—oh, my God, that was fucking ridiculous, there was *nobody* in there, there was nobody else on the *entire goddamn planet* for thousands of kilometers—

Auris squeezed her eyes shut. "I'm cracking up," she muttered; the sound of her own voice, thin and faltering under the roaring of the storm outside, was not reassuring. "I'm cracking *up*, I've got to get back to the ship—" Except she couldn't. Not until the storm subsided.

Click. Thud.

Auris's eyes jerked open. She was already facing the crew cabin, had recognized the sounds already—the sound of the cabin door latch disengaging, of the door panel sliding back. The split-second, overwhelming flood of relief roaring through her—*I'm* not *crazy! Not crazy after all!*—immediately turned into the blankest of shock as a man she didn't know stepped through the doorway, heavy dark eyebrows quirked up and a faint smile creasing his cheeks beneath his beard.

It simply wasn't possible for there to be *a man she didn't know*—

But there he was. Her eyes stung, staring—she realized distantly that she hadn't blinked once since he'd emerged from the crew cabin. The man, the *stranger,* took two quick steps forward, and it was all Auris could do not to stumble back, away from him. "Auris?" His voice was strong, resonant, easily drowning out the distant screaming of the storm outside. "Auris Delleray?"

Yes—her lips had formed the word, but with no breath behind it; all she had done was mouth it. Undeterred, the stranger stepped closer. Auris lunged sideways for the console, fingers scrabbling madly for the big red emergency beacon switch—then felt hands grab the back of her head by her hair and the console suddenly rushed up to her face, *into* her face, and the world was lost in an explosion of crushing agony.

Gliese 581g ("Zarmina"), Terraform Monitoring Station Alpha: 2181-02-08-1600

Casey Taurua stared down at the main console's shattered surface, at the ominous dark stains between the cracks in the glass that whoever had cleaned up the mess hadn't managed to entirely eradicate. She was very glad that they'd already taken Auris's body away—Auris's *body!* She shuddered all over. A hand touched her shoulder; she jerked away from it, then laughed a little, self-consciously. "Sorry, Richard—I guess I'm a little jumpy."

"No worries, I would be too. I mean, I *am,* of course." The *Mary Jackson's* senior science administrator folded his arms across his chest. "Auris, of all people, losing it down here—I always thought she got off on the solitude, honestly."

"We don't know that's what happened," Casey protested. "She wasn't showing any signs of the whatever-it-is, *paranoid agoraphobia* that Dr. Micale's been diagnosing in other people, before she left the ship—"

"Yeah, but how else could *that* have happened?" Richard jerked his chin at the buckled remains of the main console screen, still roughly indented in the shape of a human head. "Micale says she could easily have had a panic attack, started running around, tripped and fell and, *wham!*" He looked ghoulishly pleased with himself.

Casey edged away from him. "I guess so." She surreptitiously rubbed at her arms; the station seemed chillier than usual. "But...are we *sure* she did this to herself? I mean, *all* by herself? It just seems so, so—

Richard stared down the length of his nose at her. "Seriously?"

"I know, but—did we even look for signs that anyone else could have been here?" Casey knew damn well what that sounded like, but felt compelled to ask anyway.

"Like who? Everybody except the four of you on station duty were up on the *Mary*, and the Coalition ship is still nowhere near the planet. And all of you down here, except Auris of course, logged conversations with the *Mary* from your stations less than an hour before—you know." He grimaced. *"But,* just to reassure you, I did have Kimber upload all Station Alpha's logs and internal facility scans. She hasn't had a chance yet to do a detailed analysis, but preliminary results seem to confirm that Auris was all by herself down here. Sorry, Casey."

Casey's shoulders sagged. "Auris *was* a little weird when I told her about the Coalition ship. I should've known something was wrong. I should've checked in on her sooner—"

"Well, speaking of the Coalition ship—not that this is a *good* thing, of course, but—" Richard dug around in his ear with a forefinger, a habit that always made Casey cringe. "The Coalition could use access to a terraform monitoring station, and I don't think anyone aboard the *Mary* necessarily wants to come back to this one. I mean if we *had* to, of course we would, but this solves that problem pretty neatly—"

"Wait, what? We're giving the Coalition a *station?* Why?"

"*Sharing*, not giving," said Richard reasonably. "It was Kimber's idea, actually—then they won't be underfoot after they get here, and we don't have tell them why it's so conveniently empty."

"Oh my God, Richard, they're definitely going to find out! Unless they suddenly stop talking to us altogether—"

"Nah. They don't radio us just to gossip, and they won't show up in person for months yet. By then people will be talking about something else." He strolled back toward the crew cabin, humming under his breath. The cabin door slid back and Kimber herself emerged, bearing a datapad and a self-righteous expression; lips tightening, Casey turned away, fixing her gaze on the Hub's inoffensive far wall.

Poor Auris! Sure, they'd all been struggling with Dr. Micale's *good old-fashioned cabin fever*—struggling a lot more than anyone had imagined they would, pre-voyage. But not like this. Not to *this* point.

A loud bang from the Hub's ceiling hatch startled her out of her brooding. She looked around in time to see Richard glancing down at his personal commlink. "Shit," he muttered, then, louder, "Shuttle pilot says a storm's incoming—Kimber! Casey, suit back up, let's go!"

It was slow going, back up the ladder that pulled down from the ceiling hatch and up into the Hub's shuttle, docked on the station's rooftop. Casey ended up last in line, behind both Kimber and Richard. As they emerged onto the station's roof, she glanced over the top of Richard's helmet at the pale, hazy blur now swallowing the jagged black mountains in the distance, then over the top of the rock formation that shielded—or had been supposed to shield—Station Alpha's comm array. From this angle, the damage to the array looked oddly precise— storms tended to heedlessly smash obstacles into random chunks, not leave them in bizarrely neat, squared-off piles. Casey squinted at the array debris, frowning. Was it possible that Auris had damaged it herself...? But how?

Her view was suddenly cut off by Richard's head; *Come on!* He mouthed frantically at her through his faceplate, and she scrambled the rest of the way up ladder after him into the shuttle. She glanced back over her shoulder one last time just before the shuttle airlock cycled shut, but the ruins of the comm array were already gone from view, lost in the billowing white roar of the storm.

Programmed
John Grey

The navigator program plots its way
by stars and planets,

calculations
worked out for the present and beyond,

while the navigator human
steers the vessel
only by what the computer tells him.

Ahead is a dark void
that only unheard unseen impulses
can decipher, define and act on.

Even his body,
like its celestial equivalent,
functions independent
of his thoughts and aspirations.

Throughout his shift.
Excitable cells
shoot off electric signals,

while he figures he can reach
for that coffee cup

just because he has a mind to.

Mission Unknown
J Alan Erwine

The ship lifted off from the dock at Mare Insularum, pushed off the surface of the moon by magnetic beams. Onboard the ship, Captain Rick Jamieson monitored his crew and the various displays that surrounded him on the bridge.

10 kilometers away, safely under the dome of Lanaberg City, dozens of government representatives of the Solar Federation watched the ship rise from the surface. Many of them shifted from foot to foot, others chewed on nails, while others simply stared. Milling about the government officials were hundreds of Lunar citizens, trying to go about their day-to-day business. To them, it was just another launch, but to the officials, it was so much more. The citizens had no idea where this ship was going, but the government officials did. Only they and Captain Jamieson knew the true mission of the SFS Lincoln. Even the captain's crew didn't know, and he wasn't the least bit eager to tell them.

Once the magnetic pulse beams had disengaged, and the SFS Lincoln was clear of the moon's gravity, Cap. Jamieson entered the coordinates of their destination.

"I'll need a fifty-minute burn, Jenkins," he said to the pilot.

Lt. Andrew Jenkins turned. "Fifty minutes, sir? Where are we going?"

Jamieson could see the concern on the young lieutenant's face, but now wasn't the time to talk about their mission. Not for the first time, Jamieson realized how much Jenkins reminded him of a younger version of himself. The young Lieutenant had dark hair, like the Captain used to have. He now realized that a few dark strands among numerous gray ones couldn't be called dark. He had gray hair, end of story. The Lieutenant also had the joyful enthusiasm on his face that the Captain remembered he used to feel. Now the Captain feared he'd become too jaded. Jamieson repressed a sigh realizing that mostly Lieutenant Jenkins reminded him of the young man he used to be, a young man he could never be again.

"We're going where the Federation tells us to go," was the only answer he could give.

Jenkins nodded, turned, and engaged the engines.

Cap. Jamieson pushed the intercom button beside him. "Sit back and relax, everyone," he said. "This is going to be a long burn."

The crew was used to working in zero or low gravities. The 1.5 G push of the ship's acceleration would be uncomfortable for most of them, but it was necessary.

*　　*　　*

"A fifty-minute burn is a pretty big thrust, Captain," his first officer, Elena Castillo, said across the table.

The Captain grunted as he continued to eat his lunch. He never liked to talk about missions when he was eating, but that was especially true of this mission.

"Wanna give us a hint as to where we're going?" she asked. He didn't even have to look at her. He knew that she'd be staring at him with those dark eyes that seemed angry most of the time, even when she was laughing.

The Captain shook his head. "State secrets." He hated keeping things from his crew, especially his first officer, but orders were orders.

Castillo stood up, reaching her full six and a half feet height, she had been brought up in the Belt, and her body clearly showed it. She looked down at the Captain. "Secrets aren't good for morale."

The Captain slammed his fork down, although slamming wasn't very accurate as they were under .25 G's. "Orders are orders, Elena. You should know that. This isn't the first time I've had to keep things from you, or from the crew."

He stared at her, noticing not for the first time that she had a very manly face, some might call her handsome, but Jamieson never found anything attractive about her, but that didn't matter, she was his first officer, and a damn good one at that, and over the years they'd

54

developed a strong friendship, and that made keeping things from her even harder.

"No," she said, "But this is the first time you've had all kinds of meetings with those bureaucrats," she almost spat the last word.

"We're military. We do as we're told."

He could tell that Castillo was about to push the argument, but a voice from behind him stopped her. "Based on trajectory and force vectors, I'd say we're heading for somewhere in the Belt, but one of the more difficult asteroids."

The Captain could tell by the accent that Ensign Edward Al Afadil had been thinking too much again. The sixteen-year old whiz kid was usually a huge asset to the Captain, but now that thinking might be more dangerous than Jamieson wanted to imagine.

Castillo turned to the Captain with a look of concern. "P..."

He cut her off with a quick glare. She nodded her head and saluted. "Returning to station, sir." It was the most formality the Captain had heard from any in his crew in a very long time, but he understood that his first officer had ascertained the mission, the danger of the mission, and the need for her to just shut up and accept it.

She turned on a heel and left the mess hall. The Captain could hear the murmuring around him, but he ignored everyone. He didn't think her voice would have carried, so most likely none of them had quite figured out what was going on, except maybe Al Afadil. Hopefully the kid was smart enough to keep his mouth shut, but the Captain had long ago learned that smart kids weren't always the brightest. A lot of times they didn't know when to keep their mouths shut.

*   *   *

The mood was light on the bridge with many of the crew telling jokes. This is what most interplanetary travel was like. It wasn't the constant thrill and danger that was portrayed in science fiction from centuries ago. No, mostly it was just sitting around doing nothing, fighting boredom.

55

"That's not my air hose," he heard from behind him, knowing exactly where the joke was headed, but before whichever crewman it was could finish the punch line, claxons began to ring and the ship suddenly lurched, throwing the captain and most of the crew to the deck. He climbed back into his seat and began to shout orders. "Report!"

"Hull breach, deck 3, section 14," Commander Castillo shouted back. "Maintenance teams *en route.*"

"Cause?"

"Unknown, sir."

The Captain scanned the bridge crew, many of them looked concerned, but none of them seemed panicked. They were a good crew, but he also knew that if any of them had figured out what their mission might be, one of them may have become a saboteur.

"Maintenance team reports it was a meteor strike, sir," his first officer said. "Automatic shielding has sealed the damage, and all crew are accounted for. Minimal damage was done."

The Captain nodded his understanding, but he silently chided himself. They were a good crew and he never should have suspected sabotage, but he knew that he wasn't happy about this mission, so why would anyone else be if they had figured it out. Sabotage might be a stretch, but he knew he might face some insubordination the closer they got to their destination.

Commander Castillo sat down next to the Captain. "I've spent my whole life out here, and I've never seen an actual meteor strike. What are the odds?"

The Captain shook his head. "I don't know. I've spent thirty years on these ships, and I've never seen one either." He looked over at Ensign Al Afadil who was watching them. "Maybe ask him," the captain said pointing at the young ensign. Laughter erupted from the nervous crew. Even the young ensign laughed.

*   *   *

The door chime to the Captain's quarters beeped quietly.

"Enter," he called.

Ensign Al Afadil entered quietly, looking around at the Captain's quarters. In the three months he'd been on the ship, he'd never once been to the Captain's quarters, and he'd certainly never expected to be invited, at least that's what the Captain assumed.

"Have a seat."

The ensign did as he was told. Ensign Al Afadil was not much more than 1.6 meters in height and rail thin with dark skin and dark eyes that seemed to take in everything. Captain Jamieson knew that the Ensign paid attention to everything and that his brain worked in ways that the captain could never hope to understand.

"Edward," the Captain said, not quite sure how his Iranian parents had come up with that name. "This ship is your first assignment, correct?"

"Yes, sir," the Ensign said, and the Captain suddenly felt a little silly for asking. The kid was only 16. Even as smart as he was, he couldn't have been in the service for very long.

"So, there may be things you don't understand about crew dynamics, correct?"

"I suppose so," he said hesitantly. "Have I done something wrong, sir?"

"No, Ensign, you haven't. I'm just worried that you might."

The Ensign's only answer was a look of confusion.

The Captain stood up and walked around his desk. He sat on the corner of the desk just a few feet from the Ensign who seemed to be getting more nervous each second that he was in the Captain's quarters. "Look, Edward, everyone on this ship knows that you're smarter than all of us, maybe all of us put together," the Captain said with a chuckle.

The Ensign obviously didn't know what to say.

"Let me get straight to it, Ensign. Have you figured out where we're going?"

Al Afadil swallowed several times. "I believe so, sir."

"Have you shared that information with anyone?"

The Ensign shook his head. "Of course not, sir. If I'm correct, you'll have enough problems once we get where we're going. I don't want to make anything any more difficult for you before then."

"Good," the Captain said. "You have a real future with the Force, young man."

"Thank you, sir," Al Afadil said, suddenly smiling.

"Back to your station."

"Yes, sir."

*   *   *

"Begin slowing ten percent every hour," the Captain said.

Lt. Jenkins paused, started to turn, and then turned back to his station. "Yes, sir."

Captain Jamieson felt the gentle push as the ship slowly started to decelerate. Almost there, the Captain thought to himself. That would be when things got difficult.

"Sir," his first officer said with alarm in her voice. "We have ships approaching fast."

The Captain was confused. They were still hours away from the rendezvous.

"They're demanding we slow and prepare to be boarded." The first officer paused as she listened to whatever else they were communicating. "They're demanding our cargo."

"Pirates?" Lt. Jenkins asked.

"Sounds like it," the Captain answered. "Power up ablative shielding and prepare all weapons."

A blast of energy passed in front of the ship, an obvious warning sign.

"Let's return their *warning* shot," the Captain said. "Fire at the lead ship, dead on."

The crew did as they were told, and the ship bucked as the main guns fired at the main ship, hitting it dead on. The ship listed to its starboard side before righting itself. The other three ships continued to advance.

"Four against one," Commander Castillo said. "Doesn't seem like good odds."

"We're still more powerful than any one of those ships," the Captain answered.

"Still not good odds," Lt. Jenkins said.

58

"The odds are 18.6 to 1 in their favor."

"Thank you, Ensign Al Afadil," the Captain said, not needing to turn to see the young officer.

"Sir," Commander Castillo said, "We have four ships approaching from an opposing vector."

The Captain shook his head. "Please, no odds, Ensign."

The Captain watched the screen as the new ships opened fire on the pirates. Whoever the new ships belonged to, they obviously weren't working with the pirates, and each of the ships packed at least as much energy as the Lincoln did...but at least they aren't firing at us, the Captain thought.

With two ships destroyed, the pirates quickly turned tail and ran.

"Give me visual on these new ships," the Captain said, "And magnify."

There were several gasps as the crew recognized the markings on the new ships. They belonged to the Belt Liberation Force.

"I guess our rendezvous came to us," the Captain said. Everyone but Commander Castillo and Ensign Al Afadil turned to face the Captain. "Stations," was all he said.

They reluctantly returned to what they were supposed to be doing.

"The ships," Commander Castillo said, "Say that they're here to escort us to Pallas."

"Set a course," the Captain said.

He could tell by looking at the back of Lt. Jenkins' head that the Lieutenant wanted to say something, but finally he entered the coordinates and the ship fell in with the other four ships. Four ships that belonged to one of the biggest thorns in the Solar Federation's side. An organization that had committed terrorist acts against the Federation and threatened open warfare if they weren't given their freedoms.

Now the Captain was supposed to try to convince them that peace was the best option. Before this was over, he and his crew might all be dead. The BLF was not always the most forgiving of organizations.

                    *   *   *

It was the first time the Captain had ever seen Pallas up close. The large asteroid was almost round, but the gravity wasn't quite high enough to turn it into a sphere as it did with Ceres, the giant of the asteroid belt, and the home of the Solar Federation's main bases in the Belt. Their escort ships guided them to the opposite side of the asteroid, where a voice over the com told them to set down on landing deck B. The Captain had the crew do as they were told. They definitely didn't need to upset their hosts; everyone knew how volatile they could be.

Once the Lincoln was on the ground, and the crew started to enjoy the .2 gravity, a plastisteel tube came out of the base and connected to the ship. As the Captain heard the locks click into place, he proceeded to the airlock.

Once all signals were green, Captain Jamieson opened the lock. Three of his "hosts" were waiting on the other side. All three were tall, obviously born in the Belt. The two standing in front looked almost like identical twins with the same blonde hair, chiseled features, and denim blue eyes. The only reason the Captain knew they weren't identical twins was because one was male, and the other was quite obviously female. Captain Jamieson knew that the BLF loved gene modification. It was rumored that they were even breeding humans that would be able to work in the vacuum of space for limited times with minimal protections, but the Captain had never actually seen the results of any of their gene modification, but given this man and woman, he was pretty sure he was looking at BLF gene mod, albeit on a small scale. The Captain hated to think what they might be capable of if they were continued to be allowed to develop such dangerous sciences.

Behind them stood another man, a couple of inches shorter than the "twins," he still towered to just over seven feet tall. While the twins had very pale skin, this man was quite dark. The Captain also noted that he was the only one with a gun, at least a visible gun. The Captain was just happy to note that the man had the gun holstered instead of drawn.

"Captain Jamieson," the male twin said, "It's such a pleasure to meet you. When the Federation said they would be sending you to talk to us, I have to admit that I was quite relieved. Your record of fairness speaks well of your character."

"Um," the Captain mumbled, not sure what to say. He'd expected to be dragged from his ship and forced into conversations he didn't want to have. He certainly wasn't expecting a warm welcome and a smile. "Um, thank you. I'm hoping that this meeting will lead to some sort of peace that will be beneficial for all of us."

"As are we," the female twin said. Jamieson noticed that their voices even sounded similar, with his being just slightly deeper than hers. "We've put together some refreshments for you and your crew if they'd care to join us before we get down to our discussions."

Captain Jamieson just nodded. None of this was going as he'd thought it would. Finally, he turned to the one guard he'd brought with him. "Go tell Commander Castillo that she and whatever crew do not have pressing duties are free to enjoy the refreshments provided by our hosts."

"Yes, sir," the guard said before quickly turning on his heel and heading off to find Commander Castillo.

The twins turned to their escort and nodded, and he too turned on his heel and left.

"Hopefully without guns, our discussions will go better," the male twin said.

"I'm certainly hoping so," the Captain said.

*　　*　　*

Obviously hopes and dreams didn't always matter. The Captain and the twins had spent the last three hours in a small room discussing, and sometimes arguing about all kinds of minutia, and so far, nothing had come of it.

"We will never accept Solar Federation rule," the female twin said.

"Even if that leads to war?" the Captain was saying for what he thought was probably the twentieth time.

Both twins sighed and sat back in their chairs. "As we've said," the male twin said, "The BLF wants peace."

"What about the terrorist attacks?"

"We don't want to use terrorism," the male twin said. "But sometimes it's the only means that is open to an oppressed people."

The Captain shook his head and started to speak, but the male twin held up his hand. "Captain, I did some research on you before you came here. You're from North America on Earth. More precisely, you're from what is still sometimes referred to as the United States, correct?"

"Yes."

"Four hundred years ago, your country declared its freedom from the English monarchy, correct?"

"Correct."

"Many of the tactics used by those early freedom fighters would be viewed as terrorist means, at least by the British."

The Captain stared; he wasn't sure where the twin was trying to go with this.

"One incident in particular sticks out to me. It was called the Boston Tea Party. Your early patriots boarded a ship and destroyed tea by throwing it into the bay, or ocean, or whatever it was. But the important part in this is that they destroyed property that belonged to the British Empire."

"Yes," the Captain said, "But that's not the same thing."

"It's a matter of perspective," the female twin said. "We oppose your government, so they say we're terrorists, but we see ourselves as freedom fighters, much as your early American patriots would have seen themselves."

The Captain sat back in his chair. This wasn't going well, and he was becoming truly terrified that he and his crew would never leave the asteroid. It was a well-known fact that BLF recycled *everything*. He didn't really like the fact that he was about to become dinner for a bunch of "freedom fighters."

"Captain Jamieson," the male twin said with more formality than he'd shown since they'd first met, and the

Captain knew that it was endgame. He really wished he'd brought some kind of weapon. "I would assume that you have enough information to take back to your government, correct?"

"I believe so," the Captain said. "It would seem that we've reached an *impasse*." He kept himself from sighing.

"It's not unexpected," the male twin said, and his voice didn't sound the least bit troubled by the developments. "We didn't think we'd find peace with one meeting, but it's our hope that there are more people like yourself in the Federation than like those in the *government*."

Captain Jamieson wasn't sure how to take that. He certainly didn't like the tone the twin had used when saying government, but in truth, he understood what he meant, and he even kind of agreed with him. "I don't always agree with the government," he finally said. "But they are the government."

"Of course," the female twin said. "You are a good soldier."

Jamieson turned slightly towards the door. For some reason, he thought that was going to be a signal for troops to rush in and take him, but the door never opened.

"Please convey everything we've said to your government, and we hope we will have a chance to speak with you again at some point in the future," the male twin said. "Guard," he called.

The same guard from the airlock came in, and the Captain was happy to note that his weapon still wasn't drawn.

"Will you please escort Captain Jamieson back to his ship," the male twin said to the guard. "Until we meet again, Captain." Both twins bowed slightly.

The guard came up beside the Captain and said, "Sir?" pointing towards the door.

Captain Jamieson walked towards the open door, still expecting to be taken into custody at any moment, but instead, he was led back to his ship.

*   *   *

Once they were headed sunward, the Captain broadcast his report to the Federation. The next day he sat on the bridge of his ship with the rest of his crew. Spirits were high, as most of them had never expected to leave Pallas once they'd landed.

"Maybe they're not so bad after all," Commander Castillo said.

"They're still terrorists, Commander," the Captain said. "But even among terrorists, I suppose there can be good people. I'm just glad to be heading back to civilization. It'll be nice to get back to Luna and be around people that genuinely know right from wrong."

"Private message coming in for you, sir," Ensign Al Afadil said.

"I'll take it in my cubicle," the Captain said, feeling even lighter in the low gravity. Civilization was going to be great. Maybe he'd even take some time off.

*　　　*　　　*

The Captain emerged from his cubicle, his face pale and drawn.

"Sir?" Commander Castillo said.

"The Federation has decided that because of the failure of this crew and the captain, we are to be reassigned for an indefinite period." The Captain could hear the resignation in his voice, but there was nothing he could do about. He couldn't believe what was happening to them. The mission hadn't been a total failure, and he wasn't even a diplomat. How could the government expect so much from him, and then blame him when things didn't go the way they wanted?

"To where?" Castillo asked.

The Captain swallowed. "We're to oversee mining operations in the Oort Cloud."

"What?" said several members of his crew.

"Set a course," the Captain said as he flopped into his chair. So much for civilization.

Do you really want to be a writer? It's a serious question that anyone thinking about entering the field of writing should ask.

In this collection of essays, prize-winning science fiction author and editor J Alan Erwine uses his usual wit and sarcasm to educate and entertain potential writers as they start their journeys.

You won't find essays about plot or character development here, but instead, you'll find 17 essays that talk about the business of writing. Erwine uses his more than a quarter of a century of experience to talk about the submission process, and more importantly, what to do with your writing and career after you've started selling.

Do You Really Want To Be a Writer? is a great source of information for the new writer as well as the experienced writer.

https://www.amazon.com/dp/B0CRK79PSV

Desolation Stroller
Denny Marshall

Ode To Our Ancestors

Beth A. Greenwood

The moon is gone,
And the sun's red,
And the world is dead,
And I am too.
Rather me than you.

We're waiting for night to begin.
For our energy to be transferred.
A tale often isn't heard about the moon and sun.
For our time is gone and amounts to none.
I would run; rebel before you become numb.

Lunar life it's called and we're longing for a moon.
Hopefully it comes soon.
To start again.
To re-upload ourselves to the sky.
To have time to answer all the what's, where's, and why's?

I thought that was what was brought to us by lunar life,
To have really unearthly time in an earth like way,
But now I feel it is what we ought not to have done,
For we have lost the moon and soon the sun.
I'm going to leave it with you now.

As -

We're all alone and gone.
Our legacy has become null and none.
Whilst the stars wink at you before you sleep,
Remember what you sow is what you want to reap,
Instead of being hoarded like sheep.

Becoming Jade by Tyree Campbell
Reviewed by Lisa Timpf

In *Becoming Jade*, Tyree Campbell takes the reader on an adventure that is part mystery, part internal journey, and part exploration of a new and bizarrely different world. We learn several things early in the story as protagonist Annae approaches, then lands on, the planet Deege. Annae is a killer-for-hire, or a mortifice. She has been hired by Pekon Magness, Director of Projects for Corporatia Construction and Maintenance, to complete a mission. Annae, unbeknownst to Magness, has an end game of her own.

Deege, the planet Annae visits to perform the assignment, is inhabited by druzies, entities that are described thus: "Humanoid in appearance, the garbless druzy came in a variety of pastel skin colors, aqua and turquoise the most common, with caps of black head hair and otherwise hairless bodies." The druzies carry around plants called moodmartins, and Magness has told Annae he believes there is some kind of symbiotic relationship between the two.

The assignment as laid out by Magness, is simple: Annae has to kill a moodmartin and capture a druzy. Annae doesn't know what Magness wants with the druzy, but if she has her way, he won't live long enough to enact his plans once the delivery has been made. Annae hopes that obtaining the druzy will enable her to get close enough to Magness to kill him, in reprisal for the role he had in the death of Annae's beloved twin sister, Ming.

Though Annae is initially confident the mission will be a quick one, she encounters unexpected obstacles. One of the biggest setbacks is the loss of her comm device, which is tossed into the swamp by a druzy. The comm device represents Annae's only way of communicating with, and entering, her space vessel. Until she finds a way to get back in, there's no point completing the assignment, so Annae decides to focus on finding out more about druzies, moodmartins, and what's really going on here on Deege.

As events unfold, the reader gets glimpses into Annae's past, including happier times spent with Ming. Annae's mental conversations with Ming illuminate the closeness of the bond the two had when Ming was alive, and illustrate Annae's difficulties letting go of the sense of pain, loss, and guilt that accompanied her sister's death. Meanwhile, in the here-and-now, Annae has her hands full trying to figure out how she's going to complete her assignment.

Deege's geography, flora, and fauna are described in sufficient detail to render them real for the reader. Deege is a different world, though not so different as to make it impossible to imagine:

> The lower trail wound through stands of waist-high reeds and vanished in the spongy premarsh. Root-bound mud threatened to devour Annae's boots, and she retreated to solid ground, surveying the marsh. It filled a depression between the glen and a long low rise a hundred meters to the south. Beyond the crest of that rise Annae, squinting against the sunlight that glistened off the water between the reed clumps, could make out the spare upper canopy of a low forest. Before her, stalks of pink flowers that rose from head-sized, floating green nodules troped toward the northeast . . .

The terms for Annae's vessel, her weaponry, and her accessories (such as glowstones, which capture heat from the sun and radiate it back out at night) add to the sense of difference.

In addition to scene-setting, Campbell's descriptions evoke emotion:

> Dusk faded past indigo, and the glowstones cast much of the glen in a spectral tangerine. All along the tree line gnarled shadows queued up, poised to exploit latent fears. Analogs of insects and birds began a fitful cacophony comprehensible only to themselves, a vibrant overture for the rest of the

night. Annae shivered in anticipation. How much longer before the druzies came out to play? And what of nocturnal predators?

Becoming Jade incorporates subtle humor as well. On one occasion, Annae reflects on her assignment: "She had only to snap the moodmartin in half like a twig. Well, it *was* a twig." On another, she notes that "Circumstances had conspired against her, and were winning."

Suspense is maintained through the story, as Annae herself faces a series of baffling encounters, making life on Deege a puzzle she needs to solve in order to survive.

There are sufficient twists and turns along the way to keep things interesting, including Annae's discovery that Magness didn't know as much as he thought he did about the relationship between druzies and moodmartins. If you'd like to find out the real story, check out *Becoming Jade*.

Order a copy here:
https://www.hiraethsffh.com/product-page/becoming-jade-by-tyree-campbell

Finders Keepers
Susan Oke

The hum of the lander's engines vibrated through the soles of Karla's boots. She re-checked her equipment belt and pulled on the gloves of her one-piece e-suit. The sound of Taiwo's laughter drew her attention back to the sparse cabin: nothing but rows of acceleration couches and scuffed lockers. The rest of the grubbers had already dropped.

'Doesn't matter where we are in the cosmos,' Taiwo said to Geb, their team leader, 'the rocks with the tastiest minerals are always a pain-in-the-arse to get to.'

'You got that right,' Geb said.

Taiwo folded her tall, supple body into the couch next to Karla.

'This is the first inhabited planet outside of the Coalition that anyone's come across in almost a hundred years,' Taiwo said, wrapping a brightly coloured scarf around her braids. Braids that hung to her waist and were woven with tiny silver beads. Braids that did not in any way shape or form comply with the regs. 'You've got to be excited about that.'

Karla gave the young woman a jaded look. 'I'd been grubbing for one of the major corps for ten years before I set foot on a pristine planet.'

Look how that had turned out. She'd been a fool back then: newly promoted to team leader with something to prove. No sentient species, according to the scans, and a tight schedule. She'd gone for the quick and dirty option. Made the corporation millions, before it all went down the pan. Now the only work she could get was with these fly-by-night sub-contractors.

Taiwo grinned at her. 'Don't look so glum. After months of grubbing boring asteroids, I want a bit of atmosphere.'

The joke tugged at the corner of Karla's mouth.

Unlike the rest of the grubbers, Taiwo had top-level quals from one of the Core universities. Not that Karla minded. Didn't matter how tough or dirty the work, Taiwo never complained. She was a breath of fresh air in the recycled stink of their battered survey ship.

'Two minutes,' Geb called out.

The wide door of the lander slid open. Hot, dry air gusted in. Visors sealed, Karla and Taiwo held on to the grabrope, dust billowing around them as the lander descended to just a few feet above the ground. With a shout, Taiwo jumped. As soon as she was clear, Karla followed. They both crouched in the swirling dust as the lander angled off to one side before accelerating up into the too-blue sky.

'The target site is 1.5 kilometres north-east of here,' Taiwo said, checking her handheld. 'Could've dropped us a bit closer.'

'Probably didn't want to contaminate the site.'

Karla watched as Taiwo moved off at an easy lope. With a sigh, she jogged along after her. At least the terrain was fairly flat, with a scatter of rocks here and there, everything a dirty reddish brown. By the time they reached the crevice, Karla was cursing up a storm. Sweat ran down her face and neck, swamped her armpits and had fired up an unmentionable itch around her crotch.

'Tight-fisted, sand-for-brains...'

'What's wrong?' Taiwo asked over suit-comms.

'Thermal regulator's died.' Karla made one last attempt to adjust the temperature in her e-suit. No joy.

'Put in a complaint,' Taiwo said, all righteous concern. 'That's a serious breach of health and safety regs.'

'Yeah, yeah.'

Not that anyone would take much notice. Trouble was, it was easy to recruit grubbers. Youngsters from the Rim worlds would do just about anything to escape their backwater lives. That's how Karla had fallen into the life: from grubbing for crops on her parents' farm to grubbing for minerals on airless rocks.

There was a faint crackle over ship-to-suit comms. 'Found it yet?'

'Approaching the site now,' Karla said.

'Get a move on. We don't want the locals catching us poking about.'

They'd snuck down to grab samples of the crystalline material that had pinged the scanners from orbit. The lab-coats were excited, said they'd never seen anything like it. While one team made nice with the locals as per the rules and regs, Karla and the rest of the grubbers had been sent to secure samples. No point wasting time talking up a contract if the Find turned out to be a dud.

The crevice stretched out of sight, a jagged scar across the landscape. It was too wide to stride over and, when she peered over the edge, surprisingly deep. On the far side sprouted a long line of what looked like bushes, their wide green leaves splayed to catch the punishing sunlight.

Taiwo's handheld bleeped. 'I've got multiple matches.' She nodded at the bushes. 'They're the nearest. The next site is about 800 metres west of here, beyond that pile of boulders.'

Karla glanced the way Taiwo was pointing. 'All right. You go check that out. I'll secure a sample here.'

Taiwo patted her sample box and headed off.

It took a precious ten minutes to find a spot narrow enough to cross. Hopping over the gap, Karla made her way back to the glittering bushes.

'You're a real beauty.' Taking out her cutters, she knelt and snipped off a couple of crystalline branches, carefully wrapping each section before stowing them in her sample box. 'But where's the rest of you?'

Orbital scans had shown a sizable deposit in the area. She recalibrated her handheld and scanned the depths of the crevice. The screen flared and then died. Karla cursed and hit re-set. The screen remained stubbornly blank.

Ship-to-suit comms crackled into life. 'Got a group of locals closing on your position. Pickup in five.'

'Yes, sir.'

Karla switched to suit-comms. 'Taiwo, looks like we've got company.' All she got in reply was an earful of static. 'Taiwo? Get your head out of whatever hole it's stuck in. We need to get out of here.'

Shouldering her sample box, Karla jogged towards the pile of boulders. The lander arrived at the same time she did. There was no sign of Taiwo.

'Get aboard!' Geb clung to the grab rope just inside the lander's open doors, one arm gesticulating wildly.

'Taiwo's not back yet.'

'She'll just have to keep her head down and wait for the next pick-up.' When Karla hesitated, he shouted, 'Get aboard now, or spend the rest of your contract in the brig!'

*　　*　　*

Dev smiled at the villagers gathered around his lander and tried another setting on the translator. Clearing his throat, he re-started his spiel. 'Hello. We are travellers,' he pointed up at the cloudless blue sky, 'from the stars.'

Blank looks, some sniggering, a smattering of unintelligible chatter. The latter was good: it gave the translator something to work with. The locals were typically humanoid, as were the inhabitants of most of the Coalition worlds, with light-brown skin much like his own. An undiscovered colony from the Scattering, perhaps? Dev appreciated the brightly coloured, knee-length dresses of the women and their equally eye-catching head-ties. The men were more sombre in loose tops and trousers in shades of dark green and brown.

All watched him with sharp curiosity.

He tweaked the setting on the translator, more to look like he knew what he was doing than anything else. Drones had collected sufficient samples for their Med Tech to approve an 'open-helmet' delegation be sent down to the planet. That hadn't stopped her pumping him full of a cocktail of anti-virals, amongst other things. He still felt nauseous.

Scan data had shown no radio, electrical or electromagnetic emissions from the planet. Population centres were relatively small and widely scattered. A low-level agrarian society had been surmised. All he had to do was reassure the locals and offer reasonable compensation for some as-yet-unspecified exploratory mining operations.

A handful of children scampered past him.

'Ah, I don't think...'

They made disappointed noises when the lander's door slid closed; the pilot clearly didn't want company. The adults were getting restless, some shouting at the children, others deciding to join their wayward offspring, examining the matt-grey metal of the lander with interest.

Dev sighed. He was a Process Technician, not a public-relations rep. His place was back in the lab analysing and cataloguing samples. It had taken months to work their way through the asteroid belt: mapping, assaying and staking their claim to rocks rich in platinum and ferrous metals, rare earth minerals and any other valuable volatiles. And then came the real bonus: a planet in the nearest star's habitable zone. It had come as quite a shock when he was called upon to play the role of liaison between the Colter Mining Corporation and the indigenous population.

'What about the CMC Rep?' Dev had asked.

As a sub-contractor, they had to have one official CMC representative onboard.

The captain had scowled. 'The Rep won't want to get his hands dirty until he's sure there's money to be made. Look at it this way, it's an opportunity to broaden your skill set. And if it comes off, you'll get a juicy bonus out of it.'

Did the captain think he was doing Dev a favour? When your father was a senior executive in the CMC, life tended to take unexpected turns.

One of the villagers shouted a question, at least it sounded like a question.

'I'm sorry. I wish I could make myself understood.'

A couple of the young men offered tentative smiles. At least they seemed to understand his conciliatory tone. Without warning, all the villagers turned to stare down the single road that ran though the village. At first, Dev thought he'd committed some kind of cultural blunder, but then he saw what they were looking at.

It was a horse. It took him a few seconds to accept that fact. What were horses doing here? So far away from the Core worlds? The stallion tossed its head as it was reined in, its mane a flash of burnished gold, perfectly complementing the russet sheen of its coat. The crystal Find was intellectually fascinating, but this horse spoke to Dev's heart. He had spent his gap-year working on a horse ranch and had found his vocation.

Not that his father had seen it that way.

A figure dressed in a dark-green hooded jacket and dust covered trousers dismounted and stalked towards the lander. They stood half-a-head taller than Dev and most of the villagers.

Fumbling with the translator, Dev began, 'Hello. We are travellers from—'

'The stars. Yes, I know.' The words were thickly accented but understandable.

'How...? I mean, are you indigenous to this planet?' There was always a chance a rival corporation had got here before them.

A long-fingered hand unhooked the cloth masking their face, revealing high cheekbones, a thin beak-like nose and dusty black skin. Green eyes stared into his. For a moment Dev felt dizzy, but the sensation quickly passed. He really needed to get out of this heat.

'In-di-gen-ous,' the man said slowly, drawing out the vowel sounds. 'No. But this is our home and you are trespassing.'

*　　*　　*

Karla frowned as she joined the other grubbers on board the squat lander. The lab-coats wanted more samples. And they wanted them now. Four more prime sites had been identified across the two major continents that dominated this world.

According to Geb, Taiwo had checked in and been assigned another site to work on. 'She'll be all right,' Karla muttered to herself. 'Probably enjoying all that blue sky.'

She busied herself checking kit, occasionally taking a surreptitious glance at the handguns strapped to the waist of both the pilot and their team leader. Looked like the stakes had changed. No one spoke on the ride down.

Three of her fellow grubbers scored for grasslands and forested areas, though the last leapt out onto what looked like an icefield. An hour later, the lander finally slowed and hovered not far from that self-same pile of dusty boulders. The barren plain rippled in the heat-haze. Karla secured her backpack and snapped down her visor. The techs had tweaked the thermal regulator of her e-suit. It was working, at least for now.

'We'll be back in eight hours,' Geb said over comms.

'I'll be waiting.' Karla jumped out, booted feet landing square on the cracked earth.

This time it was grapple hooks and abseiling. She lowered herself carefully into the crevice, her visor adjusting to the dimming light. The crevice widened as she descended, the walls receding on either side until she was hanging in mid-air. Secure in her harness, she kept a firm hold of the brake rope as she eased her way down. Now that she was out of the glare of the sun, she could see narrow beams of light arrowing into the depths.

'Is that what you're doing?' she murmured, remembering the wide crystalline leaves and the way they angled to catch the light.

The floor was a mass of smooth ridges, the remnants of an ancient lava flow. The narrow beams of light she'd spotted intersected with a cluster of crystal rods growing about knee-height from the ground. On closer inspection, Karla realised the rods were grouped into threes with a bulbous section at the base of each set. The rods of those in the centre of the cluster were as thick as her arm, those nearer the edge were smaller, with the smallest boasting rods the length and width of her fingers.

They all pulsed with a jade light.

Karla recorded images of the overall configuration of the crystals before taking her chisel to the smallest example. She strove to separate it from the others without snapping any of its three rods. The lab-coats wanted undamaged specimens and she would get a bonus if she could deliver. Once she had it safely swaddled in her sample box, Karla circled outwards, making a careful study of the rocks. The cavernous space in which she stood gradually narrowed at each end into a pitch-black tunnel. She could waste hours stumbling around in the dark and having nothing of value to show for it.

'Which way, my lovely, which way?'

It was only when she was out of range of the wash of jade light that she spotted silvery lines in the rock floor. They led from the crystalline formation into the left-hand tunnel. Karla smiled and turned on her helmet torch. Half an hour later, she stepped inside a huge vesicle—a bubble-shaped space created by gasses escaping from free-flowing lava—and gaped. Pebble-sized crystals were embedded all across the rock's curved surface, each one pulsing with a soft jade light. The silvery lines converged on a much larger crystal, about the size of her fist, embedded at head height in the rock wall.

'I reckon you're the one they want,' she said, shrugging off her pack.

She would need a diamond-coated drill bit and a great deal of care. Karla did not want to risk bringing the whole vesicle crashing down around her.

*　　*　　*

Dev faced the tall stranger. 'Ah, hello. I am a representative of the Colter Mining Corporation. I'm here to—'

'I am Seeker Deryn. You like my horse.'

It was a statement, not a question.

'Yes. Very much,' Dev stuttered as he watched a small boy lead the magnificent animal away.

'Nki Flame Horses are a superior breed. The best on Ghyllach.'

'Ghyllach,' Dev repeated, 'Ah, the name of your planet?'

'Exactly. Our planet.' He gestured towards a single-storey building. 'Come. We will talk.'

Inside was dim but surprisingly cool. A small square table had been set with a pitcher and two glasses.

Seeker Deryn strode past the table to the corner of the room, stripped off his jacket and plunged both hands into a large bowl of water. Dev watched, bemused, as the man rigorously washed his face and neck, splashing water in all directions. With a satisfied grunt, he dabbed his face dry on a thin towel.

Devoid of dust, the man appeared younger, early thirties maybe? He wore a sleeveless vest under the jacket and both arms were encased, wrist to elbow, in an elaborate lattice of metallic strips. There was something oddly feather-like about the man's long black hair, but it was the circlet set with a jade-coloured crystal that caught Dev's attention. The most unique Find in a century and they wore it as jewellery?

'Sit.' Seeker Deryn waved a hand at the chair opposite as he took his own seat.

Dev did as he was told. It was hard not to stare at the crystal. Flecks of light danced at its core, faint at first and then brighter, sharper, before fading back into a dizzying swirl. He dragged his gaze away and watched as the man filled both glasses with what appeared to be clear water. Seeker Deryn drank with obvious relish and then waited, staring across the table. Hesitantly, Dev raised his glass but only touched the rim to his lips. While nothing obviously dangerous had been detected in any of the samples, he had been warned not to ingest anything while down on the planet.

To break the silence, Dev asked, 'What does your title signify?' Seeker Deryn just stared at him. 'Ah, I just wondered... what is it that you seek?'

'The truth, of course.'

'Ah yes, the truth.' Dev cleared his throat. 'If you're not indigenous to this planet, where did your people come from originally?' And more importantly, how did they get here? Detailed scans of the planet had detected no evidence of advanced technology.

'The Gate Keepers gifted us this planet. It is a training.... no, a testing ground. Once we have proven our worth, they will return and claim their wayward children.'

'The Gate Keepers?'

Seeker Deryn frowned. 'In your words... "gods" is the nearest.'

Religion. No way was Dev getting tangled in that. Time to change the subject.

'Your grasp of Lesti, the common language across the Coalition, is excellent.'

'I was granted the knowledge by another traveller of the stars.'

'Another traveller?' Was that why the locals were so tight-lipped? Were they in negotiations with a rival corporation?

'Yes. Different to you. Taller. Darker. A rival family, perhaps?'

How long did it take to learn a language from scratch? Even implant-to-implant it took a few days for the new dataset to settle in and translate into spoken words.

'Perhaps,' Dev replied, fighting down a surge of panic. 'But I would like you to listen to our offer before making any final commitments.'

'What is it that you seek on Ghyllach?'

'The Colter Mining Corporation is interested in rare minerals. They would pay you for the rights to investigate—'

'Investigations that you are already carrying out?'

'I'm sorry, what do you mean?' An awful sinking feeling travelled through Dev's chest and settled in his gut. The captain wouldn't do that. It was against all the rules. 'I can assure you,' he stuttered, 'the Colter Mining Corporation would never contravene—'

Seeker Deryn shook his head and tutted as if admonishing a child.

'It is time for the truth.'

*　　*　　*

She almost had it. The rock around the fist-sized crystal had been reduced to a soft crumble. Now all she had to do was... Karla eased her chisel into position and gave it a gentle tap. Jade light lanced around the vesicle, setting off a cascade of pulses from the mass of crystal nodules embedded in the surrounding rock. Squinting against the flashing lights and the solid ache that had been building behind her eyes over the last two hours, Karla repositioned her chisel: a couple more taps should do it.

A blaze of light and a sudden punch to her chest sent her staggering backwards.

'What the...?'

Straightening, she advanced on the crystal, chisel and hammer at the ready. The air seemed to shimmer; a high-pitched whining vibrated against her visor, worming its way into her skull. And then she was on her knees, fighting the urge to vomit. It'd been years since she'd had one of her 'killer' migraines. It wasn't going to stop her now.

Karla lurched to her feet and took an unsteady step towards the blazing crystal. She laid a gloved hand on its surface, fingers hooked to grab and pull. The high-pitched whining shifted into a scream... fear, anger, defiance... battered at her, through her, burrowing deep inside. She recognised that pain. Understood it. That didn't save her.

When Karla came to, she was lying on her back staring up at a starfield of muted jade nodules. Groaning, she rolled over and fought her way to her feet. It felt as though she'd been kicked in the head, repeatedly. Swearing under her breath, she checked the time: barely an hour until pick-up.

'No way. That can't be right.' She'd been out cold for nearly three hours?

The fist-sized crystal flickered, silver sparks dancing in its heart. She approached it carefully. It was now so dim in the vesicle she was forced to switch on her helmet-torch. The soft, crumbling rock around the crystal had been replaced by a grey metallic substance. It looked for all the world as if someone had come in and welded the cursed thing back into place. Out of time, Karla quickly repacked her tools—she would be penalised if she lost the drill—and stomped out of the vesicle. She patted her sample box; at least she had one thing to show those lab-coats. They didn't need to know about the migraine, or her collapsing on the job. No way she was giving them any excuse to cancel her contract or wriggle out of paying the bonus she was due.

*   *   *

Dev blinked and tried to raise his head. He was sitting at a table, or more accurately slumped, cheek pressed to its surface, drool dripping off his chin. When he did manage to sit upright, he was rewarded by a thumping headache. His eyes refused to focus on his surroundings. For a moment he was back at university, the morning after the graduation party, plagued by a monster hangover. Slowly, his overturned glass shifted into focus, followed by the low-ceilinged room. Not his student room. Not the university. Not, he realised with a sickening lurch, anywhere within the Calestis Coalition.

With a groan Dev staggered upright, the chair tipping back and clattering to the floor. Where was Seeker Deryn now? And what, by all the Scattered, had they been talking about? He had to tell the captain... tell the captain... a rival corporation! That was it. That's why Seeker Deryn could speak Lesti. That's why the man had... had drugged him?

The door wasn't locked. The village looked deserted, but the lander was still there. Dev stumbled at a half-run, barely aware that the sun had lost most of its power. The pilot was slumped in her seat; she opened her eyes and groaned as he sagged into the co-pilot's chair and activated comms.

The captain would know what to do.

*   *   *

Karla sat in the cramped mess hall along with the other grubbers and waited for Geb to spit out whatever news was giving him gut ache. Her Find had been practically snatched out of her hands. The rest of the grubbers on her drop had come back empty, one with a lurid story of being chased by monstrous wolves.

'We've got word competition is closing in,' Geb said. 'This is a major Find. One of the biggest. We can't let another corporation get in ahead of us.'

A low murmuring filled the mess-hall.

'Don't worry,' Geb said. 'Captain's sending a squad down with us to watch our backs. We'll focus on getting the site secured and the requisite contracts signed-off.' He turned to Karla. 'Karla, you'll lead the team of grubbers.'

She nodded, a sudden unease creeping through her gut. The last time she'd been in charge, all those years ago, she'd wiped out a whole ecosystem. Not on purpose. She'd been too keen. In too much of a hurry. The corporation didn't complain at the time, but once the media got a hold of the news, they couldn't drop her fast enough.

'And I'll be coming along,' announced the Rep, 'just to make sure correct procedures are followed.'

Someone groaned. The rest of the assembled crew kept their expressions carefully neutral. The Rep was as smarmy as they come: black haired and blue eyed, thought he was a real looker. Kept to his cabin most of the time, when he wasn't propositioning the younger members of the crew. But he could cancel their contract and put them all out of work with one call to the CMC.

'Well?' Geb demanded. 'Get to it. We leave in thirty minutes.'

The lander was crowded, conversation muted. Their first port-of-call turned out to be an abandoned village where they picked up their impromptu Liaison Officer. He fumbled his way along the aisle, face shiny with sweat, kiss-curls of black hair plastered to his forehead. She heard a muffled groan as he dropped into the empty couch just in front of her.

Karla settled back as the lander took off. She closed her eyes and imagined the look on the others' faces when she led them into the vesicle. They could grub out all the crystal nodules, but that fist of a crystal was hers.

*   *   *

Dev saw the dust plume before he saw the horses. A whole herd by the looks of it, racing across the desert, chasing the lander's shadow. A smile touched his lips. He pulled out his handheld and tried to capture the russet-gold blur of movement, but the lander soon outpaced the herd.

83

'Now there's a sight I didn't expect to see,' said a voice behind him.

Dev turned and peered at the woman. 'Horses, yes. I can't believe... I mean I hope they don't...' He struggled to articulate both his wonder and his concern, his thoughts scattering like startled birds.

The woman's expression softened. She had one of those square-jawed faces, hair regulation short, a touch of grey at her temples.

'The corporation is only interested in the crystals. No money in horse flesh.' She gave him a tight smile. 'I'm Karla, by the way.'

He frowned and then remembered. 'Dev. I'm Dev.'

'Yeah.' Now she looked worried. 'You been checked over?'

'The Med Tech gave me and the pilot the all-clear. I'm here to carry out an initial analysis on the samples as you bring them up.'

'Right. Us grubbers will get your crystals. Then you can get to work.'

Dev nodded. Getting back to what he knew, what he understood. Ore samples didn't ask questions; ore samples didn't turn your mind upside down looking for answers. That thought fluttered and vanished.

'Yes, back to work.'

As soon as they landed, Dev did exactly that, finding a kind of solace in the hands-on physical effort of setting up his mobile lab. Most of the crew, except the security squad, had their helmets retracted, snatching the chance to breathe real air. Dev pulled in an appreciative lungful as he cracked open the third crate; he'd take hot and dusty over the recycled stink of the ship any day.

'Riders approaching. North-North-West,' someone shouted.

Dev turned to look but could see nothing beyond the heat-shimmer that played across the rocky landscape. The security squad took up position along the narrow crevice, then dropped to one knee, rifles aimed and ready. Their sharpshooter settled on his belly on top of the lander. The horses came to a thunderous stop about a hundred metres away, on the other side of the crevice. It took a minute or so for the dust cloud to settle. When it did a line of seven figures faced them, all in dusty hooded jackets, faces masked against the desert wind. A short distance behind them gathered another ten or so, all similarly garbed.

One of the hooded figures step forwards.

'I am Seeker Deryn. I represent the Nki Family who own this territory. I formally refute any claim the Colter Mining Corporation thinks it has on this land and ask you to depart.'

Dev flinched. Just the sound of the man's voice set off a whirlwind inside his head.

The Rep smiled condescendingly. 'It's too late for that, I'm afraid. You carried out a malicious and unprovoked attack on our Liaison team. You have forfeited all rights to an open and equal negotiation.'

Seeker Deryn glanced at Dev. 'Your Liaison Officer and I had a full and frank discussion about the ethics of secretly sending in workers to steal precious crystals while supposedly negotiating for permission to carry out a survey.'

Dev shrank back behind the crate. Was that what they'd talked about? Why couldn't he remember? It made no difference. 'Just sign the contract,' he muttered.

It was better to be a live 'employee' of the CMC than anonymous 'collateral damage'. There was always a chance they could take their case of unlawful coercion to the Coalition's Core Exec. Dev gritted his teeth, hating himself for hoping the locals would just capitulate. He didn't want to find out if he was brave enough to stand as a witness against the corporation.

The Rep was saying something about Coalition law and the 'Finders Keepers' clause that allowed them to lay claim to the planet. In practice it was much more complicated than the Rep was making out. Dev shifted his attention to the horses: a shimmer of russet gold against the barren landscape. Were they in the line of fire? He edged along behind the pile of unopened crates until he was out of sight of the rest of the crew. A few strides away lay a pile of boulders marking the edge of the crevice. And beyond that, far too close for his liking, around twenty horses milled around in a loose group.

Dev was moving before he realised he'd made a decision. Crouching low, he ran for the boulders. The crevice was a longer jump than he liked, but he pulled in a breath and went for it. The horses started away from him, huffing in alarm, but they did not scatter.

*   *   *

Soft jade light filled the inside of the vesicle. Karla ignored the exclamations of the other grubbers as she approached the fist-sized crystal. This time she'd brought a laser-cutter, too bulky and unwieldy for their earlier snatch-and-grab, it was perfect for the job.

'Give me a hand setting this up.' Karla glanced at the others as they got to work. 'Be careful,' she warned. 'Remember, there's no profit in digging up dead grubbers.'

The laser sliced through rock, severing the silvery trails that converged on the fist-sized crystal. Karla felt a twinge of doubt; those silvery trails ran from the rod-like crystals in the tunnel—an energy conduit, she'd guessed. What would be the effect of cutting through—?

The rock beneath her feet trembled and then bucked. The laser toppled, gouging a ragged line across the rockface, narrowly missing slicing off a grubber's foot and cracking open one of the crystal nodules. It felt like a spike had been driven through Karla's temples. Her team were staggering around, heads in hands. The high-pitched whine drilled into her skull, her teeth, her bones. Eyes squeezed almost shut, she glimpsed the fallen laser melting a hole near the base of the vesicle. Unpeeling one hand from her ear and turning off the laser's power unit was one of the hardest things she'd ever done.

*   *   *

Arms outstretched, Dev raised his voice, 'Get out of here. Go on. Go!' The horses jostled, snorted, but refused to budge. Dev strode towards them, making shooing motions. 'You're in the line of fire. You've got to get out of here.' The horses shied away from him, but then cut in behind. Dev was surrounded. 'By the Scattered,' he murmured, 'you are the most beautiful creatures I have ever seen.' He pulled out his handheld, flicked it to record and turned a full circle. 'Why won't you just go?'

'Because I asked them to stay.'

Dev whirled around at the voice. Beyond the ring of horses, a hooded figure stood watching him.

'You have to move them out of range of the rifles.' Dev glanced up as one of the horses nuzzled at his hair. 'They're in danger here.'

'They like you.' The voice sounded amused.

One of the horses whinnied sharply. A distant rumble became a roar as the ground shifted beneath their feet. And then the horses were off, galloping back the way they had come, kicking up dust, the sound of their hooves lost in the tumult.

'I have sent them to safety.' The hooded figure crouched, one palm pressed flat to the ground. 'I sense pain... grief.' Green eyes met his. 'What have you done?'

*   *   *

Karla stumbled along the tunnel, helmet-torch cutting a wavering path through the darkness. 'The crystals are alive,' she muttered. 'More than that. They know. Understand.'

She'd heard it. Felt it. The outpouring of grief when that crystal nodule had shattered. That piercing bite of loss. Just like when her little brother died.

'Didn't know.' She raised her voice, shouted. 'I didn't know!'

Not that that would make any difference to the blazing fist of crystal back in the shattered vesicle. The gale force wind that had swept her brother off the cliff hadn't known, hadn't cared.

There were other grubbers in the tunnel.

'Call in,' she ordered over the suit-comms. She leant against the wall, listened to the trembling voices, ticking off her responsibilities one by one.

*   *   *

Dev followed the hooded figure back towards the crevice, fighting for balance on the shifting ground. The quake gradually eased into an angry rumble and then into

87

an expectant silence. The seven hooded figures still stood defiantly facing the rifles. As one they removed their jackets, revealing forearms wrapped with metallic strips twisted into complex designs; each figure was crowned with a circlet mounted with a glowing jade crystal.

'What are they doing?' Dev asked.

'Teaching,' His companion pulled off their mask and jacket. Dev couldn't hide his surprise. The woman fixed him with clear green eyes. 'Stay here with the Healers. I have a lesson to deliver.'

She left to join Seeker Deryn. Most of the remaining hooded figures were on their knees, both hands pressed to the stony ground, brows furrowed in concentration. Could they sense what had happened in the caves beneath them?

Speaker Deryn shouted across the crevice, 'You have desecrated a Nest! Killed one of our precious alphas!'

The Rep scowled. 'You abducted one of our employees, Taiwo Abeni. We are within our rights to use reasonable force to ensure her release.'

That got Dev's attention. He liked Taiwo. Not that he'd ever spoken to her, but he'd heard her talking and laughing in the mess hall. She laughed a lot, an easy laugh that made you feel included, even if you were sat at the other side of the room.

The Rep raised a hand to signal the security squad. 'You will release Taiwo, right now, or you *will* be fired upon.'

One of the figures tore off their hood and rushed forward, arms waving. 'No, don't—'

A shot rang out.

Dev would have recognised that voice and those braids anywhere. Seeker Deryn got there first. Cradling Taiwo in his arms, he didn't even glance up when Dev fell to his knees beside him. Taiwo's eyes fluttered open.

'You've got to tell them. Deryn saved me from a rockfall. I owe him my life.' She pulled in a ragged breath. 'Dev, they're telepaths! I shared…shared my thoughts, my memories.' Her eyes closed, but she was still breathing.

'Please, Seeker Deryn,' Dev kept his eyes fixed on Taiwo. There was no way he could meet that man's gaze. 'We can heal this injury, but we've got to get her back to our ship.' Blood pulsed from the wound in Taiwo's side. 'We've got to hurry. There's not much time.'

'We will care for her.' Another masked figure gently prised Taiwo from Seeker Deryn's arms and laid her flat on the ground. The person placed their hands over the wound and closed their eyes.

'Praying isn't going to help,' Dev said in desperation.

Seeker Deryn stood up. 'It's time to finish this.'

'You can't. Please. Look at what they did to Taiwo.'

Seeker Deryn marched right up to the edge of the crevice. Dev hurried after him.

'Taiwo's here,' Dev shouted. 'You shot her. Put down your weapons before you shoot someone else.'

'Get out of the way, you idiot!' the Rep yelled back.

'No. They didn't kidnap her. They saved—

Seeker Deryn slammed into Dev, knocking him to the floor. The air cracked with the sound of a gunshot.

'What kind of family murders its own children?' Seeker Deryn whispered in Dev's ear. Or were the words inside his head?

Dev scrambled to his knees. 'No,' he rasped, 'No. You can't fight these people.'

Gunshots shuddered through the air. He half expected to be surrounded by bleeding corpses. Instead, he was kneeling behind Seeker Deryn and his companions: their arms were outstretched, fingers curled into claws. He watched in amazement as an invisible force wrenched the rifles out of the hands of the security squad, who stared as their weapons arced away from them, falling harmlessly into the crevice.

The metallic mesh that encased the arms of Seeker Deryn and his companions spat and sparked with what looked like the remnants of an electrical discharge. Their jade crystals blazed like alien suns. From the samples studied in the lab, Dev knew the crystals could store solar energy. That the locals could use that same energy as a weapon came as quite a shock.

There was shouting confusion on the other side of the crevice. It was hard to make out what was happening.

Geb stepped forwards. 'I don't know how you did that.' He glanced down into the crevice. 'But I want to thank you for not killing these men.'

'The dead do not learn. The dead cannot repent.' Seeker Deryn's gaze swept over the dazed crew. 'Bring out your corporate representative. I have words for him.'

There was some scuffling around the lander's open doorway, but the Rep finally emerged, pulling at his jacket to hide his rumpled appearance. He managed a weak sneer.

'Wilful damage of corporate equipment—'

'You will be silent and listen.'

The Rep shut up. A wise choice.

'You will leave this planet immediately,' Seeker Deryn said.

'There is still the matter of the abduction—' the Rep started to say.

'I was not abducted.'

Dev spun around, torn between shock and an immense sense of relief as Taiwo stepped forwards. She looked a little unsteady on her feet. But she *was* on her feet.

'I was not abducted,' she repeated. 'I was trapped in a rockfall while carrying out an illegal assay of this planet's crystalline deposits. These people saved my life,' she touched her hand to the hole torn into her jacket by the bullet, 'more than once.'

'Perhaps we can come to some sort of arrangement?' The Rep wheedled.

Seeker Deryn scowled. 'We invoke the right to apply for membership of the Calestis Coalition.'

Gasps went up at that. Once the Coalition had you in its sights, the only safe route was to join the club. Negotiations could take years, but as an aspiring member you had 'protected' status.

'I recognise that right and stand as witness.' The words leapt out of Dev's mouth, seemingly of their own volition. He felt his face flush as the Rep and the rest of the crew turned to stare at him.

'As do I,' declared Taiwo.

She put an arm around Dev's shoulder. He stood straighter and returned the glare of the Rep.

*   *   *

Karla sat in Med Bay, enjoying being fussed over. She'd come out of it all as a kind of hero. All the grubbers were singing her praise. After all, it was she who had stopped the laser bringing down the entire vesicle on their heads and she'd got all of her team out in one piece. She thought about the handheld stored amongst her kit, the handheld that Dev had slipped to her before she'd boarded the lander. The recordings it held were patchy, with some electromagnetic damage by the looks of it, but there was enough evidence to strip the corporation of its mining licence and force it to shell out billions in compensation. If it came to light. The Rep had promised her a juicy payoff, enough to live out her retirement in comfort—after she'd given evidence as a corporate witness, that is. He'd suggested a farm, in some nice, out-of-the-way corner of the Coalition. The idiot.

Taiwo and Dev had opted to stay behind on the planet. The corporation was more than happy to leave them there; it was one way to keep them quiet.

Karla swung her legs off the bed and pulled on her coverall. Past time for a change. No more grubbing for her. She smiled. The corporation needed a good hard slap. And she was just the person to give it to them.

Settlers on Yorkin

John Grey

The landscape is
as smooth and white
as trillium petals.

But we'll survive.
Prosper even.
For the soil
is eminently fertile.
Crops pop up
like worshipers
in the church of
their own colors.
Seeding, growing, harvesting —
the planet is shocked to life.

From the first landing site,
settlements spread out
like water from a spill.
Green and blue and yellow,
and any other hue
are called on to defy
the plainness around them.
Ours is one dwelling of so many.

When the world is a canvas like this,
is it any wonder that the pioneers
paint themselves into place,
use every smudged square of palette.
From above, it's a patchwork.
From below, it's the color of your eyes.

Who?

Lisa Short is a Texas-born, Kansas-bred writer of fantasy, science fiction and horror. She has an honorable discharge from the United States Army, a degree in chemical engineering, and twenty years' experience as a professional engineer. Lisa currently lives in Maryland with her husband, youngest child, father-in-law, two cats and a puppy. She is a member of SFWA, HWA and Codex, and can be found online at lisashortauthor.com and on Twitter and Instagram @Lisa_K_Short.

MM Schreier is a classically trained vocalist who took up writing as therapy for a mid-life crisis. Whether contemporary or speculative fiction, favorite stories are rich in sensory details and weird twists. A firm believer that people are not always exclusively right- or left-brained, in addition to creative pursuits Schreier manages a robotics company and tutors maths and science to at-risk youth.

Recent publications can be found in The Molotov Cocktail, MetaStellar, and Flash Point Science Fiction. Additional listings can be found at: mmschreier.com/publications.

Eric Del Carlo's fiction has appeared in Analog, Asimov's, Clarkesworld and many other publications over the years. His latest novel, The Cold, has been released by White Cat Publications. He makes his home in his native California."

John Grey is an Australian poet, US resident, recently published in Stand, Washington Square Review and Rathalla Review. Latest books, "Covert" "Memory Outside The Head" and "Guest Of Myself" are available through Amazon. Work upcoming in the McNeese Review, Santa Fe Literary Review and Open Ceilings.

Elana Gomel is an academic and an award-winning writer. Born in Ukraine, she has lived and taught in many countries, including the US, Israel, Italy, and Hong Kong. She is the author of six non-fiction books and numerous articles on subjects such as narrative theory, posthumanism, science fiction, and serial killers. As a fiction writer, she has published more than a hundred fantasy and science fiction stories, several novellas, and five novels. She is a member of HWA and can be found at <u>https://www.citiesoflightanddarkness.com/</u> and on social media

J Alan Erwine lives just outside of Denver with his amazing wife and their youngest daughter. Yes, J is now old enough to have two adult daughters. J's family shares their household with two cats, and a turtle that pretty much keeps to himself.

J has published more than 60 short stories, three novels, and numerous short story collections. A few years ago, J realized that although he loved the small press, he couldn't make enough money writing for them, so at that point, he took control of most of his work, and has been publishing mostly independently ever since.

J is the managing editor at Nomadic Delirium Press, and in addition to writing and editing, J has also taken an interest in creating role playing games. He is the co-creator of the *Ephemeris Science Fiction RPG*, and the creator of the *Rocks on the Other Side* and *Battle for Turtle Island* RPGs.

To learn more about J, visit his website at www.jalanerwine.com or visit his blog at jalanerwine.blogspot.com.

Susan Oke says: I am a science fiction and fantasy novelist and short story writer. In my spare time, I work as the Review Editor for the BSFA REVIEW (the online magazine of the British Science Fiction Association). I am an active member of the Milford Speculative Fiction Group.

Lisa Timpf is a retired HR and communications professional who lives in Simcoe, Ontario. When not writing, Lisa enjoys organic gardening, bird watching, and taking long walks with her cocker spaniel-Jack Russell mix Chet. Lisa's speculative fiction has appeared in *NewMyths,Home for the Howlidays, Cosmic Crime*, and other venues. Lisa's collection of speculative haibun poetry, *In Days to Come*, is available from Hiraeth Publishing. You can find out more about Lisa's writing at http://lisatimpf.blogspot.com/.